"So, was chasing a mugger your idea of how the evening would go?"

"Well, you have to admit it wasn't a run-of-the-mill date," Susan commented.

"No," Brian said, "there was nothing run-of-the-mill about it."

Something about his tone hollowed out her belly. She looked up. Time seemed to stand still. She was acutely aware of the cicadas singing in the trees, of the moonlight dappling the lawn, of the scent of recently mown grass and the last of the summer roses in her neighbor's yard, but mostly she was aware of Brian.

Their eyes met and held.

He's going to kiss me.

Dear Reader,

No matter what the weather is like, I always feel like March 1st is the beginning of spring. So let's celebrate that just-around-the-corner thaw with, for starters, another of Christine Rimmer's beloved BRAVO FAMILY TIES books. In *The Bravo Family Way,* a secretive Las Vegas mogul decides he "wants" a beautiful preschool owner who's long left the glittering lights and late nights of Vegas behind. But she hadn't counted on the charms of Fletcher Bravo. No woman could resist him for long….

Victoria Pade's *The Baby Deal,* next up in our FAMILY BUSINESS continuity, features wayward son Jack Hanson finally agreeing to take a meeting with a client—only perhaps he got a little too friendly too fast? She's pregnant, and he's…well, he's not sure what he is, quite frankly. In Judy Duarte's *Call Me Cowboy,* a New York City girl is in desperate need of a detective with a working knowledge of Texas to locate the mother she's never known. Will she find everything she's looking for, courtesy of T. J. "Cowboy" Whittaker? In *She's the One,* Patricia Kay's conclusion to her CALLIE'S CORNER CAFÉ series, a woman who's always put her troublesome younger sister's needs before her own finds herself torn by her attraction to the handsome cop who's about to place said sister under arrest. Lois Faye Dyer's new miniseries, THE McCLOUDS OF MONTANA, which features two feuding families, opens with *Luke's Proposal.* In it, the daughter of one family is forced to work together with the son of the other—with very unexpected results! And in *A Bachelor at the Wedding* by Kate Little, a sophisticated Manhattan tycoon finds himself relying more and more on his Brooklyn-bred assistant (yeah, Brooklyn)—and not just for business.

So enjoy, and come back next month—the undisputed start of spring….

Gail

Please address questions and book requests to:
Silhouette Reader Service
U.S.: 3010 Walden Ave., P.O. Box 1325, Buffalo, NY 14269
Canadian: P.O. Box 609, Fort Erie, Ont. L2A 5X3

SHE'S THE ONE
PATRICIA KAY

SPECIAL EDITION®
Published by Silhouette Books
America's Publisher of Contemporary Romance

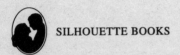

SILHOUETTE BOOKS

ISBN 0-373-24744-3

SHE'S THE ONE

PATRICIA KAY,

formerly writing as Trisha Alexander, is the *USA TODAY* bestselling author of more than thirty contemporary romances. She lives in Houston, Texas. To learn more about her, visit her Web site at www.patriciakay.com.

Chapter One

The blinking message light on her phone was the first thing Susan Pickering saw as she walked into the kitchen of her small bungalow at nine-thirty that night. Dropping her purse, her tote and her bag of take-out Chinese food on the kitchen table, she headed for the counter where the portable phone sat in its base.

Sighing—Thursdays were always such long days— she keyed in the code for her voice mail and rubbed the back of her neck while she waited for it to kick in. At least sales had been good today. Some Thursdays it hardly paid to keep the shop open until eight-thirty.

"You have two new messages," the canned voice said. "Press One to listen…"

Susan pressed One.

The first message was from the president of the women's club at Susan's church with a reminder of the board meeting that would take place Monday night. Susan was the club's secretary.

Since Susan already had a note on her calendar about the meeting, she deleted the message.

Then the second message began.

"Ms. Pickering. This is John Mellon with Allmark Visa. Please call our 800 number regarding your overdue bill. Failure to call will mean immediate cancellation of your card and all privileges."

He went on to give her the complete phone number and, before hanging up, urged her once more to call immediately, saying their customer-service department was open twenty-four hours a day.

Susan frowned. What in the world was he *talking* about? She hadn't used her Allmark Visa card in at least six months, and there was no balance the last time they'd sent her a statement. Susan didn't believe in using credit cards unless it was absolutely necessary. In fact, she only owned two of them—the Visa and her American Express card.

There must be some mistake. There *had* to be. She dug her Visa card out of her wallet because she knew they would want her account number. Then she pressed in the keys for the 800 number. It took awhile before she was connected to a person. She had to wade her way through the automated answering system first, but after making three or four selections, she finally had a live voice.

"This is Esther. May I have your account number?"

Susan slowly gave the woman the number.

"Um, is this Ms. Pickering?"

"Yes, this is Susan Pickering."

"Would you give me your mother's maiden name, please?"

"Newman." She spelled it out.

Silence.

Susan's frown deepened.

"Um, Ms. Pickering, I'm going to connect you with someone in the business office. Please hold."

Before Susan could utter a word of protest or even ask a question, the line went silent, followed by the soothing sounds of easy-listening music. Except, Susan was too rattled to be soothed by anything, unless she heard the words "We're so sorry for the mix-up, Ms. Pickering, there's obviously been a terrible mistake."

After what seemed like an eternity, a youngish male voice came on the line. "Miss Pickering?"

"Yes?"

"Miss Pickering, this is Robert Wiley. Are you calling to make a payment?"

"Look…Mr. Wiley, I don't know what you're talking about. I haven't used my card for months. I don't owe you anything. You must have me mixed up with someone else. Why, I haven't even received a statement from you in at least six months."

"That's impossible. We've sent you at least three communications regarding your outstanding bill in the past month alone and they haven't been returned."

His implication was that she was lying, which got Susan's hackles up. "Well, I'm sorry, but I didn't receive them. Maybe you sent them to the wrong address. Anyway, I told you. I haven't used my Allmark Visa card in at last six months, so I can't imagine why you're sending me statements, anyway. Maybe you've charged someone else's purchases to my card by mistake."

"According to the address change you requested, we have your address listed as…" He proceeded to give her a post office box address in Columbus, which was thirty miles from Maple Hills where Susan lived.

Susan began to feel like Alice in *Alice through the Looking Glass*. This whole thing was just *bizarre*.

"First of all," she said, "I never sent you an address change. Secondly, I still live on Fifth Street in Maple Hills, not Columbus, in the same house I've occupied for eight years. And…I hate to sound like a broken record…but I haven't used my card in six months, at least."

Susan was mad now. Allmark had screwed up, but she could see it was going to take her many phone calls, e-mails and wasted hours clearing up this mistake, even though none of it was her fault.

Dammit, anyway.

Why hadn't she canceled that card when she'd thought about it a couple of months ago? If she had, she wouldn't be having this aggravating conversation, especially tonight, when she was exhausted from her eleven-hour day at the antique shop and wanted nothing more than a glass of wine and her Chinese food.

"You're saying you didn't call us on…the tenth of June…with an address change?"

Again she heard the skepticism.

"No, I didn't," Susan snapped. "It must have been someone else and another card and you people got them mixed up."

"Pardon me, Ms. Pickering, but that's impossible. Anyone calling to change an address would have to give us all the particulars on the card involved including correct address, phone number, card number, social security number and mother's maiden name. Now if it wasn't you who charged over $6,500 on this card, who was it?"

"Sixty-five hundred dollars!" Susan was shocked. She couldn't remember the limit on that card, but she was sure it wasn't more than eight thousand. "Ohmigod. I…I can't imagine."

But a tiny kernel of anxiety had knotted in her stomach, even as she expressed her ignorance.

Could Sasha be responsible for this?

Oh, God. Surely not. Susan's younger sister had been in trouble many times, but she'd never broken the law…. Well, unless you counted her drug use.

And don't forget that one time she shoplifted.

But she was just a teenager when that episode happened. And that incident had taken place during her worst and most rebellious period. Susan reminded herself that Sasha had never done anything like that again.

She wouldn't have done this to me, would she?

No.

Sasha wouldn't.

She *wouldn't*.

There was another explanation for this credit card problem, and it didn't involve her sister.

"S-someone must have stolen my identity," she said, grasping the first option that came to her mind: this doesn't involve Sasha.

Finally the man she was talking to sounded sympathetic when he said, "I'm sorry, Miss Pickering. If what you say is true, then it looks as if you're the victim of credit card fraud. I'll turn this over to our fraud division, and they'll be calling you."

"What about all the charges on my account? Am I liable for them?"

"If everything checks out, you won't have to pay more than fifty dollars."

Susan sagged against the counter in relief. She didn't know what she'd have done if they'd insisted on more. Her business bank account had a fairly healthy balance of five thousand dollars, but she couldn't keep her doors open if she let it get too far down.

And her personal account was pretty low right now because she'd just paid for some expensive dental work. That was one of the drawbacks of owning a small business. She couldn't afford gold-standard health insurance or dental insurance.

"I advise you to notify your local police, because this might not be an isolated incident," he said. "It's possible your identity *has* been stolen."

Susan closed her eyes. *I do not need this hassle right now*.

Susan made him repeat the post office box address, which she wrote down, and she gave him the fax number at the shop so he could fax over copies of the statements showing all the purchases which had been made.

"I'm curious about something," she said. "I made a rather large purchase on this card right after I got it, and I remember someone from your company called me the next day to make sure I really had made the purchases. They said it was a safeguard against someone else using the card."

"Yes, we do that," he said.

"Then why didn't anyone call me about all *these* purchases?"

"We only call when an individual purchase is more than $500…or when a person's buying history warrants a call. In your case, none of the charges against your card were individually large. In scanning over them, I see that the largest was $365 at Banana Republic."

Susan bit her lip. Banana Republic. Sasha loved shopping there. But Sasha couldn't have done this. She couldn't. Susan refused to believe it. It had to have been someone else.

"Thank you," she finally said. "I'll call the police as soon as we hang up."

"It can wait until morning," he said. His voice was now kind. "We put an alert on this card more than a month ago, so whoever's been using it won't be able to use it again."

"Okay."

"My shift will be over in about fifteen minutes. But tomorrow morning, if your local police want to call us, they can talk to Bob Blackstone. He's the head of our Fraud Department. I'll send everything over to them before I leave here tonight."

"Okay," Susan said again, writing down Balckstone's name.

When they hung up, her head was spinning.

She wondered if Ann was home yet. A member of Susan's Wednesday-night gang—they all met for a weekly dinner at Callie's Corner Café on the Maple Hills village green—Ann O'Brien was Susan's best friend. But tonight Ann, a real estate agent, had been invited to go to the symphony by a grateful client and she'd told Susan she probably wouldn't be home before midnight.

Susan looked at her watch. It wasn't quite eleven yet. The conversation would have to wait until tomorrow. That was probably for the best, anyway. She was so tired right now, she probably wouldn't make any sense. *She'd better get to bed*. Especially since she needed to get up fairly early so she could go to the police station and make her report in time to arrive at the shop by nine-thirty.

Hazel's Closet, the antique shop her mother had opened after the death of Susan's father, was now Susan's livelihood. It was also her passion.

She'd never imagined, when she took over the shop, that she would grow to love it so much. When her mother died of breast cancer eight years earlier, Susan was a manufacturer's rep for office products and furniture. She worked sixty-hour weeks and traveled constantly. There was no way she could continue the kind of work she was doing and still be there for Sasha, who was only eleven. So Susan resigned her position, moved back into the family home and took on the job of mothering Sasha, while learning the antique business.

At least one of those endeavors has been success-ful, she thought with a grimace.

When Sasha graduated from high school, Susan had hoped she would want to work with her at the shop. But Sasha quickly informed her she had no interest in working there. She told Susan she wanted to model. She was certainly beautiful enough; she definitely had the look.

Susan sighed again, remembering how her sister

had finally worn her down. Susan had reluctantly withdrawn Sasha's portion of their mother's life insurance money to stake her sister in New York while she tried her luck at modeling. It only took six months for her to come back to Ohio—all the money gone.

Since then she'd held a succession of pie-in-the-sky jobs, which she kept quitting—or, as Susan suspected, getting fired from.

Susan knew she made too many excuses for Sasha's behavior, that she had enabled her irresponsibility by not insisting she suffer the consequences of her actions, but Susan couldn't seem to help herself. She felt guilty that Sasha had grown up without a father and that their mother had died when Sasha was so young. She kept thinking if she'd been a better "mother" to her sister, Sasha would have turned out differently.

Sometimes Susan felt so alone. If not for her girlfriends—especially Ann—she wasn't sure she would have survived all the tough years.

But things with Sasha were looking up. Recently she'd been hired to manage a small apartment complex in nearby Banning and seemed to really like the job. She'd bought herself a used car, and when they'd last talked, she was even talking about taking some computer classes at the local community college.

Maybe the bad times were finally behind them.

With that hopeful thought, Susan got up, turned

off the TV, took her dirty plate and wineglass into the kitchen, then got ready for bed.

Tomorrow she would go to the police and put this unpleasantness about her credit card behind her, too.

The next morning Susan pulled into the parking lot of the Maple Hills Police Station on the dot of eight. She felt unsettled and nervous, which frustrated her, because she hadn't done anything wrong.

She slowly climbed the shallow concrete steps leading to the main entrance of the red brick building. The station had been built in 1922, and Susan knew from reading a recent article that there were fifteen total employees, which included everyone from officers to the dispatcher to the janitor. She only hoped one of them would be able to help her.

Once inside she approached the uniformed duty officer—a big man with a short, military haircut— who sat behind the front counter. He looked up from a log of some kind. "Yes? May I help you?"

"Hi. I'm Susan Pickering. And I need to talk to someone about possible identity theft." She went on to explain her problem.

"Have a seat," the officer, whose name tag identified him as Sergeant Riggs, said. He pointed to some wooden chairs lining the front wall. "Someone will be with you soon."

Susan leafed through a dog-eared copy of *U.S. News and World Report* while she waited. About ten minutes later she was approached by a big, good-looking man with short black hair and striking blue eyes.

"Miss Pickering?" he said. "I'm Lieutenant Brian Murphy. C'mon back. We can talk at my desk."

He opened the swinging door at one end of the counter and stood back, letting her precede him. Then he led the way through an inner door, which opened into a large, bull pen–type area with half a dozen desks. On one side of the open area were several holding cells, two of which had occupants. On the other side were a couple of offices with large windows. Susan guessed the chief of police probably rated an office.

Only two of the desks were occupied—one by a young blond man, the other by a redheaded woman with a telephone headset on.

"That's Jamie, our dispatcher," Brian Murphy said. He inclined his head toward the redhead.

Reaching the last desk on the right, he indicated a side chair, saying, "Have a seat." Then he sat behind the desk. "Would you like some coffee? Or a soda?"

Susan shook her head. "Thanks, but I'm fine."

"Okay. First I'll need to get some information from you." He reached into one of the trays on his desk and pulled out a form.

After Susan had given him all the required information, he asked her to tell him exactly what had happened.

So Susan explained her problem again, telling

him everything she'd been told. Throughout, he listened, nodding his head several times, and writing down information.

"Did you check your other credit cards?" he asked when she'd finished.

"The only other credit card I have is my American Express, and I checked my account online. There's nothing charged on the card other than the purchases I made this month. I keep pretty close tabs on that card because I use it for groceries and gasoline. It's a good way to keep track of what I spend."

He nodded again. "What about your Visa card? Do you always keep it in your wallet?"

"Yes."

"And is your wallet always with you?"

Susan shook her head. "No. When I go out in the evening, I usually take a small handbag. My wallet doesn't fit in it, so I just take my American Express card and some cash with me."

"So your wallet is left at home?"

"Yes."

"Has anyone besides you been in your home when you've been out in the evening? A babysitter, maybe?"

"No, I don't have any children."

"What about relatives?"

Susan hesitated. "Well, my sister lived with me for a couple of weeks a few months back, but I'm sure she had nothing to do with this." But even as she said this, she could see the skepticism in the lieutenant's eyes. *He's wrong. This can't be laid at Sasha's door.*

"Have you talked to your sister about this?"

Susan shook her head. "No, I haven't." In fact, she hadn't talked to Sasha in more than two weeks. Although she hated to admit it even to herself Sasha only called Susan when she wanted something. Susan *had* tried to call her a few days earlier, but when Sasha didn't answer, she didn't leave a message.

"What about when you're at work? Is your card with you then?"

"Yes."

"Is it possible someone could have gotten hold of your wallet at work?"

"The only other person who would have access to my purse is my assistant, and I'd trust her with my life."

"What's your assistant's name?"

"Look…I know she's not involved."

His blue eyes met hers. "I still need to know her name," he said softly but firmly.

Susan sighed. "Gerri Mullins."

After writing it down, he asked, "What about your statements? Do you shred them?"

"No, I'm afraid not." She grimaced. "I've been meaning to get a shredder. I just haven't gotten around to it."

"Yeah, I know," he said kindly, "it's one of those things we put off doing."

It was nice of him not to make her feel guilty.

"You know," he said now, "it is possible that someone stole a copy of your statement from your trash and that's how they got hold of your account number."

"Really?"

"Sure. Happens all the time."

Susan felt better. She'd been right. Sasha wasn't involved in this. It was Susan's own carelessness that had caused the problem. She thought about how her trash sat out for hours before it was picked up. And she was at work all day, so anyone could have let themselves into her side yard and gone through the bags without anyone seeing them.

"But what about knowing my mother's maiden name? That's not information that appears on my statements."

"There are many public places thieves can get that kind of information once they know what to look for—birth records, marriage records…"

Susan bit her lip. "I'll go buy a shredder today."

"Good." He opened a drawer of his desk and pulled out a sheet of paper and handed it to her.

Susan saw that it contained instructions pertaining to identity theft as well as the telephone numbers of the three credit reporting agencies in the U.S. "Do you think my identity has been stolen, then?"

"I don't know. But you need to find out, and this is the way to do it. The credit reporting agencies will be able to tell you if any new credit cards have been issued in your name that you didn't apply for."

Susan swallowed. She was almost afraid to know.

"Call me after you've gotten the reports and we'll go from there." For the first time since he'd introduced himself, he smiled. "Don't look so stricken. We'll get this cleared up. And if the credit card company gives you any guff, have 'em call me."

Susan felt an enormous sense of relief just in knowing that Lt. Murphy didn't think she was a deadbeat trying to pretend she didn't run up her Visa bill, that he believed her and that he was on her side.

She returned his smile. "Thank you. I feel better already."

After Susan Pickering left the station, Brian couldn't get her out of his mind. He kept thinking about how she'd sat there twisting her hands while she talked, how her eyes had filled with uncertainty when he'd mentioned her sister, how she kept her gaze trained on his without wavering and how she'd hung on every word he'd said.

Even if she hadn't told him her marital status, he'd have guessed she wasn't married, because she wore no wedding ring—although that wasn't a dead giveaway. His sister Aileen didn't wear a ring because she was allergic to gold. Still, the fact he'd almost immediately noticed Susan Pickering's lack of a ring perplexed him.

She was the first woman to spark his interest in a long time. Why was that? Sure, she was pretty, with her shiny brown hair and soft brown eyes, but there were a lot of pretty women out there that hadn't interested him.

It was something about those eyes, he decided. A certain vulnerability. Almost an expectation that whatever news she was given wouldn't be good. That told him Susan Pickering's life hadn't been a bed of roses.

But hell, whose life is?

Just then, his phone rang. He looked at Jamie, who mouthed, *It's your ex*.

Most divorced men cringed when their ex-wives called, but Brian and Lonnie had a good—some might even say a great—relationship, and Brian knew all the credit for that belonged to her. She could have been a bitch when he'd asked for the divorce.

Instead she'd done everything in her power to make sure everything remained as friendly as possible. He knew the main reason was she didn't want their daughters to be any more upset than they already were, but Lonnie also loved his family. She and his sisters were thick as thieves, had been from the moment he'd made her his wife.

Brian knew he was lucky.

Picking up the phone, he said, "Hi, Lonnie."

"Hi, Brian. Listen, I'm stuck at work, and the school just called to say Janna threw up in class. Is there any chance you can go get her and stay with her until I can get home?" Janna was their twelve-year-old.

"Sure, no problem."

"I'll call Sarah, see if she can come and fill in." Lonnie was a nurse and worked for a family practitioner.

"Okay. If she can't, I'll take her to Mom's."

"Please don't, Brian. I don't want to constantly depend on your mother to bail me out."

"You know she doesn't mind."

As a matter of fact, Sheila Murphy would probably cut off her right arm if Lonnie asked her to. Brian would never forget how, when he and Lonnie were married, his mother had said, "If you two ever split up, we're keeping her." She'd said it in a kidding way, but Brian had known she was halfway serious. His parents adored Lonnie. Always had.

"I know," Lonnie said, "but I don't want to take advantage of her."

"Let's not worry about that now. I'll go get Janna. Call me on my cell when you know what you're doing."

After they hung up, Brian grabbed his jacket and walked over to the chief's office. The door was partly open, and the chief was sitting at his desk reading.

"Chief?"

Chief Harvey looked up. "Yeah, Brian?"

"Janna's sick. I need to go pick her up at the school. Then I'll be at Lonnie's until she can get home. If Jack Polito calls, tell him to call me on my cell, okay? I'll get back here as soon as I can." Jack was with the county coroner's office.

"Sure, no problem. You *did* remember you're supposed to go over to the high school at three?"

"Yeah, I remembered." Brian was talking to the freshman class today about the dangers of drug use and what to do if they were approached by a dealer. "Don't worry, if Lonnie can't get away in the next hour or so, I'll take Janna over to my mother's."

"Okay."

That was one of the good things about working for a small-town police force; you were part of a family instead of just a cog in the wheel.

Ten minutes later Brian pulled into the visitors' parking lot of the Maple Way Middle School where Janna was in the seventh grade. Ten minutes after that, he and Janna were on their way.

"So you threw up, huh?" he said.

"Yeah," she said, making a face. "It was gross, Dad."

He smiled. He adored his youngest daughter. He knew you weren't supposed to have favorites, but although he loved his daughters equally, he secretly admitted to himself that he enjoyed Janna more.

Kaycee, at fifteen, could be difficult. In fact, most of the time she was. Even Lonnie, who was one of the most even-tempered people Brian had ever known, sometimes lost patience with her.

"I think it must have been something I ate," Janna was saying.

"For *breakfast*? What did you have?"

"Leftover pizza."

"Oh, jeez, Janna, it's no wonder you got sick. I'm surprised your mom let you eat that cr—er, stuff for breakfast."

Janna made another face. "Um, she didn't know."

"She didn't *know?*"

"Nuh, uh. She was upstairs drying her hair. She thought I was eating Cheerios."

Brian grinned. "Janna…"

"I know."

"I hope you learned a lesson, peanut."

Heaving a sigh, she said, "Yeah. No more cold pizza for breakfast."

By now they'd reached the two-story red brick house Brian and Lonnie had bought fourteen years earlier. It still gave Brian a twinge to realize he would never live in it again. But it had only been fair to let Lonnie have the house in the divorce settlement. After all, the kids lived with Lonnie, and this was their home.

Besides, you felt so guilty about wanting out of the marriage that you'd have given her anything.

That, too, he thought wryly.

Maybe that most of all.

Anyway, this situation wouldn't last forever. Once the kids were out of the house, he and Lonnie had agreed they would sell the house and split the money.

He sighed. Dissolving a marriage was complicated. Hell, *marriage* was complicated. If only he'd loved Lonnie the way he should have…

He wondered if Susan Pickering had ever been

married. Then he wondered why she'd popped into his head again.

He frowned. There was no sense thinking about the Pickering woman. Because no matter how attractive she was, he knew he wouldn't do anything about it.

Even if he wanted to, he had nothing to offer a woman. The divorce had left him drained, both financially and emotionally. It had been three years now since he and Lonnie had split, and he was still trying to adjust. And even if a woman *was* interested in him, he wasn't sure he had the energy to do his job well, give his daughters the attention they needed, help his parents—his father had Parkinson's disease—and also sustain a meaningful relationship.

It would take a very special and understanding woman to put up with all the crap in his life, and he wasn't sure a woman like that existed.

Regretfully he said a mental goodbye to thoughts of Susan Pickering.

From now on she was just another case.

Chapter Two

Susan always tried to be at the shop by nine-thirty, even though she didn't officially open until ten. She liked that quiet half hour when the phone didn't ring and she could slowly get ready for her day.

This time of year was a busy one for her. She always held a customer-appreciation sale the second week of September, after the kids were back in school. The sale lasted a week and, combined with the sales for the last two weeks before Christmas, accounted for more than forty percent of her gross income for the year.

This year's customer-appreciation sale would begin next week, and Susan was spending any down time going through her inventory and trying to decide which pieces she wanted to discount and move out before the summer shows, when she always found things she wanted for the shop.

Unfortunately, right now her store was just about maxed out in terms of space, so if she brought in anything new, she had to make room for it. The other option she'd been considering was to move to a new, larger location, because over the years she'd learned that, if she bought wisely, most pieces would eventually sell without her having to lower the asking price. It only took the right buyer.

Susan would never forget the "sleeper" her mother had found at a flea market. Hazel Pickering had suspected the figurine was valuable, much more valuable than the $150 price tag. She'd bought it and, after cleaning it up, knew for certain it was a rare Hummel *Eventide* with the original crown marking. She'd priced it in the five-thousand-dollar range *Shroeder's Antique Price Guide* suggested.

The piece sat for nearly a year; even the two diehard Hummel collectors who would ordinarily buy anything Susan's mom found shied away from the asking price. Susan remembered how her mother had considered lowering it, yet hadn't.

And then one day a woman who lived in Cleveland but was visiting Maple Hills happened to come into the shop. She'd taken one look at the figurine and bought it on the spot.

It definitely paid off to have enough space to

keep good pieces as long as it took for the right buyer to show up.

On the other hand, Ann and the other members of her Wednesday-night gang had been encouraging her to take the money it would cost to move and instead invest it in a online store.

"The Internet is the wave of future," Ann insisted. "It's completely changed the way we do business at the agency. Instead of us having to run listings of houses for people to look at, they can go online, look up the areas and houses that interest them and eliminate the ones they don't want to see. Saves us hours and hours of time."

Susan knew all that. Shoot, she used the Internet all the time. She'd love to have an online store as well as expand her physical location. Unfortunately, right now she couldn't afford to do either one.

She swallowed.

What if she discovered her identity *had* been stolen? That thousands and thousands more dollars had been spent in her name? What if she ended up being liable for some or all of it? What would she do?

Don't think about that now she told herself. Maybe the Allmark Visa card is an isolated incident. Remember what Mom always said about not borrowing trouble.

Pushing the frightening thought out of her mind, Susan headed back to the tiny kitchen area located in the storeroom in the back and put on the teakettle. Her mother had begun the tradition of serving tea and scones throughout the day, and Susan had continued it. Nowadays the scones weren't homemade— Susan didn't have her mother's bent toward baking—but she'd found a supplier on the Internet and kept enough in her freezer so that she didn't have to reorder more than four or five times a year.

As she readied herself and the shop for the day ahead, she couldn't stop her thoughts from going to her visit to the police station. Even though she was scared to find out the depth of her problem, she was grateful for Brian Murphy's help and advice. He had been so nice to her, and it had been a tremendous relief to see that he'd believed her. No wonder she'd liked him.

Be honest. That's not the only reason you liked him.

Susan smiled sheepishly. She'd always been a sucker for big, dark-haired men, and the lieutenant had certainly filled the bill. Yes, she'd found him very attractive. Those blue eyes alone were striking enough, but combined with his size, his warm smile and his dark hair, he was close to being a ten.

She wondered if he was married. He hadn't been wearing a wedding band, but that didn't mean anything. Lots of married men didn't wear rings. Yeah, but she'd also noticed a framed photograph of two young girls on his desk.

Susan sighed. Those were probably his kids and he was probably married. All the good guys were. She made a face. Wouldn't you know that the first man she'd had this kind of immediate attraction to in more years than she cared to count would be unavailable?

At thirty-three Susan was beginning to wonder if marriage and children were in the cards for her. When she was younger, she'd just naturally assumed that eventually she would meet someone and fall in love and get married. After all, wasn't that the normal course of events? And then her mother had died, and her whole life had changed. Instead of being a carefree single woman with a job that afforded her opportunities to meet lots of other young people, she took over the responsibility of raising her sister and became the proprietor of a small antique shop in an equally small town.

She'd quickly discovered there weren't many eligible men in Maple Hills. Oh, she hadn't been dateless the past eight years. She'd gone out with men she'd met through friends and one she'd met at an antique show in Columbus, but none of them had created a spark, and after a couple of dates the relationship—if you could call it that—had fizzled out.

Susan wanted to be married. She especially wanted children. In fact, she wanted the whole deal—the Hallmark family that you saw in those sweet commercials, the kind of family she'd had for too short a time. But she was beginning to despair of that ever happening.

And yet, sometimes romance *did* come along, even for women over thirty-five. Look at Zoe, she thought with a smile. Zoe Madison, now Zoe Madison Welch, had met the love of her life at the age of forty, despite all of the experts with their depressing statistics about women who hadn't married by the time the first blush of youth faded.

As she walked to the front of the shop, turned the Closed sign to the Open side and unlocked the door, Susan wondered exactly what the odds might be for that sort of lightning to strike twice.

At ten o'clock, Susan called each of the three credit reporting agencies. To her great relief, nothing untoward appeared on her record. The only bad mark against her was the report from Allmark Visa showing that she was behind in her payments.

Just to be on the safe side, Susan asked all three agencies to flag her name and notify her immediately should anything new show up.

Then she called Brian Murphy to tell him what she'd found out.

"Lieutenant Murphy is out right now," the woman who answered the phone said. "Would you like to leave a message?"

"Yes, please."

Once that was done, Susan called Ann at her office.

"Are you *sure* Sasha had nothing to do with it?" Ann asked after Susan told her about the credit card mess.

Susan knew it was her own fault that Ann immediately suspected Sasha *could* have done this, because Susan had certainly done her share of complaining about her sister the past few years. And yet it hurt Susan that Ann would think Sasha capable of such a horrible betrayal.

"I know Sasha's done a lot of things that are less than admirable," she said, fighting to keep her voice from revealing her emotions, "but I can't imagine she'd ever do anything like this to me."

"I'm sorry, Susan. I shouldn't have said that."

"Look, I understand why you might think it. Sasha hasn't exactly been the model of responsibility in the past."

Susan couldn't help remembering the time when Sasha was eighteen and had just graduated from high school. Susan had had to go out of town for an antique show. When she returned two days later, she found the house trashed and Sasha, along with some guy Susan had never seen, naked in Susan's bed. Susan had been furious.

Afterward, Sasha had apologized tearfully saying it would never happen again. Susan had chosen to believe her because she'd seemed so sincerely sorry.

Shaking free of that depressing memory, Susan turned her attention back to Ann and what she was saying.

"Have you called the credit agencies yet?"

"Yes, and thank goodness there was nothing else."

"That's a relief."

They talked a little more, with Susan telling Ann all about her visit to the police station.

"Tell me more about this Lieutenant Murphy," Ann said, a teasing note in her voice.

"Why don't you pick up a couple of salads—I'll buy—and come and have lunch with me? I'll tell you all about him then."

"If you don't mind waiting until one, I will. I've got a closing at eleven and it might last awhile." Ann's sigh was clearly audible. "This is that couple I told you about. The ones who gave me so much trouble over that foundation problem."

Susan had long ago decided there was no way she would ever have the patience to be a real estate agent. Buying or selling a house ranked right up there in the top five or six things that caused the most stress in a person's life, and Ann's clients certainly reflected that.

Of course, Susan thought ruefully, Ann made a lot more money than Susan did, so perhaps the rewards were worth the aggravation and lousy hours. For that was another thing Susan would hate—the way Ann had to work every weekend.

"One o'clock is fine," Susan said.

After hanging up, Susan stood there thinking. Before she could change her mind, she pressed the speed dial for Sasha's cell phone. After four rings, Sasha's voice mail kicked in. Frustrated, Susan almost hung up. After all, she'd already left Sasha a couple of messages. Then she changed her mind.

"Sasha, this is Susan. Please call me when you get this message. It's very important. *Very important*."

Then she disconnected the call.

In between the half-dozen or so customers who stopped by or called the rest of morning, Susan busied herself with her list of items to mark down more than the fifteen percent discount all her customers would receive during her customer-appreciation sale week.

She was standing in front of a display case containing Johnson Brothers turkey plates and platters when the bell announcing a customer tinkled. Turning, she was startled to see Brian Murphy walking in.

"Oh, hi," she said, smiling. Putting down her clipboard, she walked to the front of the shop.

His answering smile was warm. "I got your message. I know you're relieved about those credit reports."

She nodded. "Yes. Very."

He looked around curiously. "You've got a nice place here."

"Thank you. It was my mother's."

"Is that where the name Hazel comes from?"

"Yes."

Advancing farther into the shop, he stopped in front of a case where there was a large display of sterling silver flatware and serving pieces.

"My grandmother loved silver," he said reflectively.

Susan smiled. Her grandmother had loved silver, too. Funny how nowadays so many people had gotten away from using silver—Susan included. It was just too much trouble to clean it, she thought sadly.

She remembered how, as a child, she would sit at her grandmother's scarred maple kitchen table with a polishing cloth and silver cream—she'd considered it a privilege to clean her grandmother's serving pieces, especially—and while her grandmother worked around the kitchen, the two of them would talk.

Sophie Pickering had been dead for more than twenty years now, but Susan still missed her acutely, the same way she missed her mother. She sighed.

Slowly he turned around to face her. "I need your sister's address."

Susan blinked. "Why?"

"I want to talk to her."

"But those statements went to someone in Columbus. Sasha doesn't live in Columbus. So she couldn't be involved."

"I'm sure you're right. But I still want to talk to her. Maybe when she was staying with you, someone visited her. Maybe that person got the information on your card and is the one who used it and changed the address so you wouldn't know for a while. There are all kinds of things that might have happened, and I need to check them out if we're going to get to the bottom of this."

That made sense. "Okay. I'll get it for you." As she walked back to her office where she'd stashed her purse, she wondered if he thought it odd that she didn't know Sasha's address off by heart. But Sasha had moved so often, Susan rarely had a chance to commit her address to memory.

A few minutes later, armed with the address she'd written on a sheet of notepaper, she walked back to where he was now standing looking at a Springfield Armory musket, circa mid-1800s.

"You like that?" she said.

He turned around. "It's a beauty."

"Would you like me to take it down so you can get a closer look?"

He shook his head. "No point. I can't afford antiques on my salary." He grimaced. "Actually, I can't afford much of anything."

Susan nodded. "I know the feeling." She handed him the paper with Sasha's address. "This is where my sister is living. It's an apartment. She's the manager of the complex."

He folded the paper and put it into the breast pocket of his jacket. "Thanks."

"Um, when you talk to her, would you ask her to call me?"

"I'll do that."

If he thought her request was odd, he didn't say so. "Thank you."

"I'll be in touch," he said. "And you let me know

if you hear anything more from the credit card company."

"All right."

Walking out, he had to pass the case where she kept the jewelry she sold on consignment. He stopped. "My oldest daughter has a birthday next week. She loves jewelry." He gazed into the case. "I don't suppose there's anything here that a kid that age might like that wouldn't break the bank?"

"I've got some beautiful brooches for under a hundred dollars," Susan said. "Brooches are all the rage nowadays."

"A brooch. That's like a pin, right?"

Susan smothered a smile. "That's exactly like a pin." She opened the case from behind and removed several of her favorite brooches. "This one…" She placed a delicate starburst brooch made out of different shades of blue stones on the top of the case. "Is $110, but I'll sell it to you for $90."

"Blue's Kaycee's favorite color," he said slowly, picking up the pin.

"This one's also lovely," Susan said, picking up a butterfly brooch studded with yellow and pale-violet stones.

"I like the blue one," he said. Then he grinned. "Okay, it's a deal." He pulled out his wallet, extracted a MasterCard and handed it to her.

Once she'd taken care of the transaction, she said, "Want me to gift wrap it for you?"

"That'd be great. Tell you what. What time do you close?"

"Tonight? At six."

"I'll stop by before then and pick it up."

Although she felt uneasy about his upcoming visit to Sasha, she couldn't help smiling after he was gone. He'd looked so delighted with the brooch he'd picked out for his daughter. But that wasn't why Susan was smiling. She had a feeling Brian Murphy was divorced. Because why else would *he* be picking out a birthday gift? In Susan's experience, in the great majority of families, the wife did the shopping, especially when it came to gifts for daughters.

Don't get your hopes up. You could be wrong.

Besides, she thought, even if she *wasn't* wrong, Brian Murphy hadn't indicated in any way that he was interested in her as anything more than a case he was working on.

Now, had he?

It took Brian forty minutes to get to Banning, a trip that shouldn't have taken more than twenty-five minutes, max. Jeez, he thought, it was impossible to drive anywhere anymore without running into road repair crews.

Finally he reached the town, and then it took him another ten minutes to find the apartment complex where Sasha Pickering lived.

Brian hadn't told Susan, but he'd looked into both

her background and Sasha's, and he strongly suspected that, despite what Susan wanted to believe, her sister might well be behind the illegal charges on Susan's credit card.

For Susan's sake, he hoped not, because even though it would be easier to clear things up if the culprit *was* her sister, he knew it would be emotionally tough for Susan to handle.

He parked his truck in one of the spaces in front of the office. A cheerful white sign identified the complex as Banning Gardens Apartments, and as if to reinforce the "gardens" part, a large bed of begonias and zinnias was planted around the sign and on either side of the walkway leading to the office door.

A middle-aged woman with salt-and-pepper hair and black-rimmed glasses sat behind a large desk. She was typing away on her computer's keyboard and kept on typing for a few seconds before looking up. The nameplate on her desk identified her as Nancy Little, Resident Manager.

"Sorry," she said. "Had to finish that before I lost my train of thought. May I help you?"

"Yes, I'm looking for Sasha Pickering. I understood she works here?"

The pleasant look on the Little woman's face was replaced with a frown. "*Worked* here. Past tense. She quit her job last week."

"I see. Does she still live here?"

"Nope. And good riddance."

Brian wasn't surprised, either by the woman's information or her attitude. He'd gotten bad vibes about Sasha Pickering even before finding out she'd once been arrested for shoplifting and had been in constant trouble throughout high school.

"She left a big mess in her apartment, too. Her and that loser who was living with her."

Brian took out his wallet and opened it to show the woman his ID. "I'm Lieutenant Brian Murphy. I really need to talk to Miss Pickering. Do you have a forwarding address for her?"

Nancy Little laughed. "That was a joke, right? Those two cleared out of here in the middle of the night. They sure didn't leave a forwarding address."

Brian wasn't surprised about that, either. "Out of curiosity, what did she do when she *was* here?"

"Answered phones, did some data entry, learned how to show apartments, that kind of thing."

"So she wasn't the manager?"

Nancy Little looked at him as if he were crazy. "The *manager*? No. She wasn't even the *assistant* manager. Although, if she'd worked out, she could have been." She shook her head. "I'll never understand these kids. Sasha is smart, but she wasn't reliable."

"Why'd you hire her?"

"That's a good question. I almost didn't because she didn't have any references. She said she hadn't worked in several years because she'd been taking care of her mother in California. I felt sorry for her. Thought I'd give her a chance."

Now Brian shook his head.

"So that was a lie, right?"

"Yes," he said, "that was a lie."

"Oh, well. Live and learn."

"What about the guy? You said she was living with someone?"

"Yes. His name was Gary. I knew he was a loser the first time I set eyes on him."

"You don't know his last name?"

"Nope. I never asked. I didn't want to get into any kind of discussion about him. I figured if I did, I might say something I shouldn't."

"What did he look like?"

"Tall, skinny, long dark hair. And he always wore cowboy boots."

"Did you ever talk to him?"

"Not if I could help it. Besides, he was one of those types who grunted instead of speaking in sentences."

"Did Sasha Pickering ever talk about him?"

"She wanted to, but I wasn't interested. Sorry."

"Well, thanks for the information." Brian took out one of his business cards and handed it to her. "If you should hear anything from her or remember anything that might be useful in finding her, give me a call."

"Okay."

As Brian drove back to Maple Hills, he wished he had better news for Susan Pickering. Because now he was almost positive her sister was responsible for the fraudulent charges on her Visa card.

He just hoped she didn't shoot the messenger.

Chapter Three

Susan was in the back of the store, trying to decide if she wanted to lower the price on a pine washstand she'd had for almost two years, when the bell on the front door tinkled announcing someone's arrival. Looking up, she saw Ann entering the shop. Susan walked up front to meet her, smiling.

"Hey," she said, "you're early." It was only twelve-forty.

Ann nodded. "For once the closing didn't take as long as I thought." She looked impeccable as always. Today she wore a chic black linen dress with white accents, black-and-white mules and, in addition to carrying their lunch, had a big black handbag with a white flower design slung over her arm. With her blond hair styled in a sleek, shoulder-length pageboy and her smoky-blue eyes accented by skillfully applied mascara and eye shadow, she had perfected how to look understated, successful and sexy all at the same time.

Susan wished she had that knack. Ruefully she glanced down at her white blouse, khaki skirt and plain brown sandals. At least she'd painted her toenails in one of the trendy new shades, this one deep burgundy. But she hadn't bought herself any new clothes in a long time. And if she didn't get this credit card mess cleared up, she might not be buying anything for the foreseeable future.

She pushed that thought out of her mind; she was tired of thinking about it.

Ann, who had spent many lunch hours with Susan, walked around and behind the L-shaped display case. Susan had her desk and computer back there, as well as a small table where she did her gift wrapping, price tagging, silver polishing and small repairs. Ann set the bag containing their salads on the table, then put her purse down on the floor and sank into the extra chair Susan kept for visitors. She immediately kicked off her shoes. "Damn things hurt," she muttered.

Susan eyed the offending mules. "No wonder. Those toes are so pointy, they're practically lethal weapons."

Ann smiled wryly. "But you have to admit they're stylish."

"That's why you're a fashion plate and I'm not," Susan said. "I prefer comfort."

"I *have* to look fashionable. It makes my clients feel secure. They think I'll get them a better deal."

Susan laughed. "I think you're just trying to justify spending lots of money on clothes."

Ann grinned. "There's that, too." She opened the bag of food and took out two plastic containers of salad and several smaller containers of dressing and croutons.

"I'll go get us some drinks," Susan said. "Want your usual diet soda?"

Ann nodded.

A few minutes later, armed with Ann's soft drink and her own bottle of water, Susan rejoined her friend. "Now, if I'm lucky, I'll get my salad eaten before another customer comes in," she said as she sat down.

"Has the morning been busy?" Ann asked. She popped the top on her drink and took a long swallow.

"Not bad. I sold some primitives, a couple of Limoges dishes and some jewelry." Remembering Brian Murphy's pleasure over the gift for his daughter, she smiled.

"What're you smiling about?"

"Nothing."

"C'mon, Susan. I know that look. You're pleased about something."

To change the subject—because Susan wasn't sure she wanted to talk about Brian Murphy yet—she said, "I am, and you will be, too. I've got a new piece of Depression glass."

Ann's face lit up. She was passionate about Depression glass and had an extensive collection. In fact, that's how the two women had met. Ann had come into the shop about five years ago, they'd begun talking, and within a year Ann had invited Susan to join the Wednesday-night gang. They'd been best friends ever since.

"What? Where is it?" Ann looked around.

Susan rolled her eyes. "Don't worry. It's in the back. I'll get it when we're done eating."

"But *what* is it?"

"You're so impatient. It's English hobnail. A cobalt-blue creamer and sugar bowl set. And it's in perfect condition."

Ann let out a breath. "I'm almost afraid to ask how much."

"For anyone else, $125." Susan smiled. "For you, $95."

"Well, hurry and finish eating so I can see it."

Susan laughed. "You're impossible." She put her food down. "I'll go get it now."

She was walking back up front with the creamer and sugar bowl set when Lucy Reinhart, one of her best customers, walked in. Handing the glassware set to Ann, Susan smiled at the woman. "Hello, Lucy."

"Hi, Susan."

"How was your trip to France?"

"It was wonderful. Just wonderful. I hated to leave."

"When did you get back?"

"On Wednesday." Glancing at Ann, Lucy added, "I'll just look around awhile. You finish your lunch, Susan."

"All right, but if you need me, just let me know. Oh, and the tea's hot, if you'd like some."

Lucy smiled. "Thank you."

"Is that the Lucy you're always talking about?" Ann asked softly.

Susan nodded. Lucy Reinhart had spent more than five thousand dollars in the shop so far that year, and Susan knew she would spend close to that much over customer-appreciation week and Christmas. In fact, she was probably now making a mental list of what she wanted to buy when the sale began at the end of the month.

"So," Ann said, "you were going to tell me about the sexy cop you met."

"Who said he was sexy?"

"Oh, come on," Ann said with a grin. "Even though you didn't, I heard it in your voice."

Ready or not, Susan guessed she was going to have to talk about Brian Murphy. "Okay, you win. He *is* sexy."

"I want details." Ann polished off the last bite of her salad and closed the lid of the plastic container, then stuffed it back into the bag. She gave a contented sigh and leaned back.

"Do you want a scone?" Susan asked.

"Quit trying to change the subject. Details…remember?"

Picturing Brian, Susan smiled. "He's tall, probably about six-three, and big, with black hair and the bluest eyes I've ever seen."

"Married?"

"I don't know. I think he *was* married because there's a picture of two girls on his desk, and one of them is the spitting image of him." Susan went on to tell Ann about Brian buying the brooch for the older daughter. "So that makes me think he might be divorced."

"That makes sense," Ann said. "But you need to find out for sure."

"How can I do that without coming right out and asking him?"

"There *are* ways, but what's wrong with asking him? When he comes to pick up the brooch, just say something like, I'm guessing you're divorced since you bought this on your own."

"Oh, God, I don't know…he'll see right through that, I think."

"So what?"

Susan made a face. "It'll be embarrassing."

Ann rolled her eyes. "But you like him, don't you?"

"Yes."

"Then get over being embarrassed. Find out if he's divorced, and if he is, flirt with him. And if he flirts back, you can drop hints that you wouldn't say no if he asked you out. If he doesn't take the hint, *you* ask him *out*."

"You know I can't do that."

"Why not, for heaven's sake? This is the twenty-first century, not the eighteenth."

"The last time I took the initiative with a man, you know what happened."

"Not every man is like Craig. This cop sounds like a really nice guy."

"I know." But Susan was gun-shy. She'd met Craig Ballard the year before her mother died, when she still lived and worked in Columbus. He'd seemed really nice, too, but he'd turned out to be anything but. On their second date he wanted sex, and when she resisted, he turned nasty, saying she was a tease and calling her any number of ugly names. Luckily, Susan had somehow managed to avert being raped, but not before getting thoroughly frightened.

When she'd refused to see Craig again, he'd become furious and begun to stalk her. She'd had to get a restraining order against him, and it had been a long time after that disastrous episode before she felt secure enough to sleep through the night.

Just then Lucy Reinhart came back up front. "Susan, I've decided I'm going to take that Sylvan butter dish and cover."

Susan smiled. Lucy had been coveting that particular piece of glass for a while now. "If you want it now, I'll give you the same discount you would have gotten during customer-appreciation week."

Now Lucy smiled, too. "Thank you. That would be great."

Susan was thrilled. The amber butter dish and cover were priced at $1,300. Manufactured in 1931, they were quite rare. Even with the fifteen percent discount she was giving Lucy, she would pocket a nice profit.

Susan's specialty was glassware of all kinds; she had an extensive inventory. Because of her expertise, she was building a good reputation and attracting buyers from greater distances. And she would do even better when she could afford to put up an online store.

After Lucy left, carrying her carefully wrapped and cushioned package, Ann whistled. "That was a nice sale."

"Like I said, she's one of my best customers."

"Listen, I definitely want this set. But can you hold it for me till next week? I'd prefer to wait until I'm paid for today's closing first."

"You know I will."

They talked a few minutes more, then Ann slipped her shoes on again and headed back to the restroom to brush her teeth and touch up her makeup.

"See you Wednesday night," she said on her way out the door. Then she grinned. "But if anything exciting happens before then with the sexy cop, you'd better call me."

Susan laughed. "You'll be the first to know."

Once Ann was gone, Susan cleaned up their trash and went back to taking inventory, but her heart wasn't in it. Talking about Brian with Ann reminded her that Sasha hadn't returned her call. Susan didn't know whether to be worried or angry. She wondered if Brian had managed to contact Sasha, and if so, what she'd said. You'd think she'd call Susan if he had. Certainly, in her shoes, Susan would have called. But Sasha had never done the logical thing. It was almost as if her brain was wired differently from Susan's.

Susan sighed. She hoped Brian would have some answers for her when he came back to collect the brooch he'd purchased. And she hoped they'd prove without a doubt that Sasha was not involved in the credit card problem.

Brian was just finishing up a report before leaving the station when Jamie buzzed him. "Ed Grayling on line one."

Brian grinned and picked up the phone. Ed was a former coworker who had retired from the force last year. "Hey, Ed, how's it going?"

"Couldn't be better. Well, no, I take that back. It *could* be better. As a matter of fact, that's why I called."

"What's up?"

"What's up is my business has taken off. I've got so much work, I've had to turn assignments down."

"That's great, Ed." Ed had gone into the private security business, opening an office in Columbus.

"Not that great. I don't like turning business down."

"Guess you'll have to hire some help, then."

"That's why I'm calling. I want you, Brian."

"Me?"

"Yeah, you. How does a job that pays you fifty percent more than you're making now sound?"

Brian blinked. "Fifty percent?"

"For starters. Plus, you'll get an end-of-the-year bonus based on profits. I haven't worked out all the details yet, but we'll nail that down in a written contract when you come to work for me."

Brian couldn't help thinking about how much easier life would be for both him *and* his kids if he earned more money. "Jeez, Ed, I don't know what to say."

"Say yes. I promise you, Brian, you won't be sorry."

"I…I've got to think about it before I can say anything. I mean, I've been on the force for eighteen years."

"Hell, Brian, I know that. I was there sixteen years myself. And no one loved being a cop more than I did. But sooner or later, a man has to think about his family. If I'd stayed on the force, there was no way I would've been able to send Mark to the kind of college he wants to go to. Nor could I help my mother. Kit and I were looking at moving her in with us, which she didn't want and we didn't want. Now I'm able to give her enough each month so she can live independently. But you know all this."

Yes, Brian did know. And he had to admit, there

were many times over the past year when he'd envied Ed. But quit the force himself? He swallowed. Could he do that? "Ed," he finally said, "I appreciate the offer. And I'm tempted. But I have to give it more thought. Quitting when I'm only two years away from full retirement benefits is a pretty serious step."

"Trust me. You'll make up the difference tenfold."

"Tell you what. Let me think about it for a few days, and I'll call you back. Then maybe we can meet for dinner or something."

"Okay. Sounds good. And, Brian? Trust me. This is the right thing to do."

For the rest of the day Susan tried to keep her mind focused on work. For the most part she was successful. It was only as it got closer to closing time that her thoughts returned to her sister and, by extension, to Brian Murphy. As soon as they did, her stomach felt unsettled.

At five forty-five, the bell on the front door jangled, and Brian walked in. Susan took one look at his face and knew whatever news he had for her, it wasn't good.

"Hi," she said, hoping she was wrong.

"Hi." His sober expression didn't change. "I'm afraid I don't have good news for you."

Susan listened with a sinking heart as he relayed his conversation with the manager of the apartment complex where Sasha had been working.

Her shoulders slumped in defeat as he finished by

saying, "I'm sorry, Susan. I know this isn't what you wanted to hear."

Susan knew what Brian was thinking. He thought Sasha was the one who'd charged all that stuff on her credit card and that she'd taken off because she was afraid of being caught. "You know, just because Sasha took off doesn't mean she's guilty of anything."

"That's true."

"But you don't believe that, do you?"

He shrugged. "All the signs—"

"I don't *care* about the signs. I know Sasha. She wouldn't do that to me. If she's involved at all, it's only because of her low-life friends."

But even as Susan was putting the blame elsewhere, she knew she was in denial, because Brian could easily be right.

Brian couldn't stand seeing that bleak look in Susan's eyes. Man, if he had that sister of hers here, he'd set her straight. What the hell was *wrong* with her that she'd do something like this to someone as nice as Susan? Brian would bet money that Sasha Pickering was the one behind the credit card charges.

He watched as Susan tried to pretend she wasn't upset, but her smile didn't quite reach her eyes.

Maybe in addition to setting Sasha Pickering straight, he'd strongly suggest she remove herself from her sister's life. Because Brian had been a cop long enough to know there were some people who were never going to be anything but trouble.

"I wrapped your daughter's present," Susan said, handing him a box done up with pale-yellow paper and curly purple ribbon.

"Thanks." He wanted to offer her some kind of assurance or comfort, but what could he say?

Just then the grandfather clock Brian had admired earlier began to chime the hour.

Susan sighed. "That's my cue. Time to close the shop."

Brian hesitated. He knew he should just say goodbye, but he felt oddly reluctant. He wondered if she had any plans for dinner.

Don't be stupid, Murphy. Whether you take that job with Ed Grayling or not, you already decided you're not in any position to get involved with anyone, let alone Susan Pickering.

But even as he told himself this, he found himself saying, "Do you like Italian food?"

She blinked. The corners of her lips turned up in a tentative smile. "I…um, yes, I love Italian food."

"If you don't have any plans for dinner, how about joining me? I'll take you to Tony's."

"I love Tony's. And no, I don't have any other plans. But—" She hesitated.

"But what?"

"I—" She seemed embarrassed. "You're not married, are you?" she blurted out.

Brian always assumed people knew he was divorced, yet how could she have known? Inwardly he kicked himself for putting her in the position of having to ask. "No, Susan, I'm not married. I was, but I've been divorced for three years now."

Now she rewarded him with a real smile. "Then I'd love to go to dinner with you."

"Great."

"I'll just be a few minutes."

He watched as she shut down her computer and tidied up. He liked watching her. In fact, he liked just about everything about her. Too bad, he thought, because this wasn't going to go anywhere after tonight. He was taking her to dinner, yes, but only because she was obviously in need of a friendly face and some assurance that the sky wasn't falling, even if her sister *had* probably betrayed her.

She took her purse out of a locked cabinet. "Be right back."

Then she walked to the back of the shop and disappeared. A few minutes later she reappeared wearing a wheat-colored jacket, and he could see she'd brushed her hair and put on some fresh lipstick. He knew Susan was thirty-three, but she looked fresh and young in her simple outfit. He wondered why she wasn't married. He'd have thought some guy would have snapped her up by now. She was obviously the home-and-hearth type.

All the more reason to stay away from her, Murphy.

They walked out into a surprisingly cool evening. Summer was over, Brian thought. He wasn't sorry to see it go. There was always more crime in the summertime. "Want to go in my truck and I'll drop you back here afterward?" he asked.

"Why don't I just follow you instead?"

"All right."

As he pulled out of the parking lot with Susan's car right behind him, Brian's cell phone rang. Reaching for it, he looked at the caller ID. It was either Lonnie, his ex, or one of the girls. He'd have to answer.

"Hello?"

"Dad?" It was Kaycee.

"Hi, honey."

"Hi. Hey, Mom has her bridge club tonight and I was thinking maybe we could go out for pizza or something."

Damn. "Honey, I wish I could, but I have something going on tonight."

"You do?" She didn't even try to disguise the disappointment in her voice. "Well, how long will you be?"

"I don't know. But it might be late."

"I guess that means Janna and I get to eat macaroni and cheese again."

Brian chuckled. "You love macaroni and cheese."

"Not two days in a row."

"Tell you what, fix a salad—and don't tell me your mother doesn't have everything there you'll need for a salad—and I'll bring a pizza by no later than eight-thirty. From Tony's," he added.

"From Tony's?"

"Yes."

"Okay, great. And, Dad?"

"Yes?"

"I love you."

"I love you, too."

Brian disconnected the call and told himself he hadn't really lied to Kaycee. He *did* have something going on tonight.

But if she had any idea he was having dinner with an attractive woman...

Hell, it wasn't like this was a *date*, or anything. But even as Brian told himself this, he was very glad Kaycee didn't know exactly what it was he would be doing for the next couple of hours.

As always Tony's smelled wonderful. And it was surprisingly crowded for so early on a Friday night. But they had no trouble getting a table. Susan knew that even thirty minutes later it might have been impossible.

After they were seated, she looked around. Inevitably, in a town like Maple Hills, and especially at a popular restaurant like Tony's, she would run into someone she knew. Sometimes several someones.

Tonight was no exception. Across the room she saw Mavis Newton and her husband, who went to

Susan's church. And a few tables over were two women who belonged to the garden club. She also saw Brian nod to several people. She imagined he knew even more of the townsfolk than she did.

"How about some Chianti?" Brian asked as their waiter approached.

Susan smiled. "Why not?"

After Brian had ordered a half carafe of the house Chianti, Susan said, "You'll have to let me know how your daughter likes the brooch."

"I will."

"When's her birthday?"

"Tuesday."

"Are you doing anything special?"

"We're having a family celebration at the house. Actually, it's my ex-wife's house now. The girls live with her."

Susan guessed that must be hard on him.

"I see them a lot, though. In fact, I'll see them later tonight. I promised Kaycee, the birthday girl, I'd bring them a pizza from here."

"Sounds like you have a good relationship with them."

"Yeah, I'm lucky. Lonnie and I, we've managed to keep the split friendly."

"That's good. It's hard on kids when their parents can't get along. And that happens too many times nowadays."

"Yeah, it does. We both agreed we didn't want to

cause the girls any more pain than was absolutely necessary."

"And are your girls okay with everything?"

"Now. But it was rough at first. They…didn't expect it. I hated hurting them."

Susan saw the regret in his eyes. *He's a good man*, she thought. *The kind of man who really cares about people.* "How old's your other daughter?"

"Janna?" He grinned. "She's twelve."

"Almost a teenager, too."

"Yeah. But Janna doesn't act like one yet, thank God."

Just then their waiter returned with their wine and a basket of hot garlic bread, a house specialty. "Are you ready to order?" he asked.

"We haven't even looked at the menu," Brian said.

"I don't need to," Susan said, "I know what I want."

Brian laughed. "Me, too. Truth is, I've practically memorized the menu since my divorce."

Susan smiled. She ate out a lot, too. Or rather, she ordered in a lot. "I'll have the tortellini and ravioli combination."

"And I'll have the cannelloni," Brian said. "And about halfway through our dinner, would you put in an order for a medium house-special pizza?"

"Sure thing," the waiter said.

Susan wondered what it would be like to marry someone who had teenagers. The thought made her uncomfortable. First of all, for all she knew, Brian was only being nice to her because he felt sorry for her. And if that wasn't his motive in asking her out to dinner, this was only a first date. There might not ever be a second. And she might not *want* there to be a second.

So just cool it.

"Do you have any other brothers and sisters besides Sasha?" Brian asked once their waiter was gone.

Susan shook her head. "It's just us. What about you?"

"I've got three older sisters."

"What about your parents? Are they still alive?"

"Yes, they're still kicking. Although my dad has Parkinson's disease, but he still functions pretty well."

"Do they live here in Maple Hills?"

"Yep. My entire family does. All my sisters are married, and they all have kids except for Caitlin, who's the closest in age to me. When we get together, there are sixteen of us."

Susan felt a stab of longing. He was so lucky to have a large family. And it was obvious, from his warm expression, that they were close. "So you're the only son. I'll bet *you* were spoiled."

A cloud passed over his face. "I wasn't the only son. I had a younger brother. He died when he was eighteen."

"Oh, I'm sorry."

"Yeah. Me, too."

"How old were you at the time?"

"Not quite twenty."

"Was it an accident?"

Brian hesitated. "Yes."

Susan knew there was a story there, but she didn't want to probe. If Brian wanted to tell her, he would.

"He overdosed on drugs."

Susan didn't know what to say.

"Our parents were devastated. Kevin was the golden boy who could do no wrong. They're still in denial over it." He sighed and stopped talking as their waiter came back carrying their salads.

"I can't imagine what it must be like to lose a child," Susan said after the waiter walked away.

"It's the worst thing that can happen to a parent."

Susan nodded sympathetically, then reached for a piece of the garlic bread and took a bite before turning her attention to her salad.

"But it was a long time ago," Brian said. "Now what about you? Were you always in the antique business?"

"No. When my mother died, I moved back to Maple Hills because Sasha was only eleven and there was no one else to care for her except me. Not that I minded," she was quick to assure him. "I love Sasha. I wanted to take care of her."

I still love her, Susan thought, *despite everything*.

"What were you doing before that?"

"I was a manufacturer's rep. I sold office equipment, furniture and supplies."

"In?"

"Columbus."

"So you were never far away."

"No." Susan cut a cherry tomato in two and put a piece in her mouth.

Brian was almost finished with his salad and was starting on his third piece of garlic bread. Susan smothered a smile. He obviously had a good appetite.

"And you really like the antique business?"

"I love it. I had no idea I would love it the way I do, but it's almost become an obsession." She forked a bite of salad. "Taking over the shop turned out to be a really good move for me. And my sales experience helped tremendously."

By now their food had come, and for a few minutes they ate without talking. Just as Susan was going to ask Brian another question, a familiar voice said, "Susan! Hi."

Susan turned to see Shawn McFarland, her husband Matt and the newest addition to their family, two-month-old Emily. "Hi, Shawn. Matt. Oh, and Emily. Look at her. She's growing so fast!"

Shawn, who Susan had always thought was the prettiest of their Wednesday-night gang, smiled happily. "Isn't she?" The pride and love on her face gave Susan a pang. Would she ever have a baby of her own?

Shawn looked curiously at Brian. "I know you," she said. "You're Caitlin's brother, aren't you?"

"Guilty," Brian said, rising. He stuck out his hand. "Brian Murphy."

Shawn shook it. "Shawn McFarland." She introduced the others, and Brian and Matt shook hands.

They talked a few minutes more, and Susan knew Shawn was wildly curious about Brian and how long Susan had known him, because usually her friends in the Wednesday-night gang knew everything about each other's lives as soon as there was anything to know.

"Nice people," Brian said when the McFarlands left to go to their own table.

"Very nice people," Susan agreed.

"That's not her first husband, is it?"

"No. Shawn and her first husband divorced several years ago, and Shawn married Matt two years ago."

"His name sounds familiar. What does he do?"

"He teaches math at the high school."

"*That's* where I heard it. Kaycee has mentioned a Mr. McFarland." Brian smiled. "She likes him. Now I see why."

Susan chuckled. "Most of the girls have a crush on him." She thought about how Shawn's daughter, Lauren, had once had a crush on Matt and how it had caused problems between her and her mother.

But everything had worked out all right, thank goodness, because if ever two people were meant to be together, it was Shawn and Matt. Susan felt envious every time she saw them; they were so obviously in love. And now they had Emily.

As Shawn always said, her cup runneth over.

"I used to have a crush on my biology teacher," Brian said. "As the kids say nowadays, she was *hot*."

Susan grinned. "And I had a crush on one of my English profs in college."

By now they'd finished their dinners, and the waiter had come to clear the table.

"How about dessert?" Brian said.

Susan shook her head. "I'm stuffed. But you go ahead."

"I'd better not. The chief keeps lecturing us about staying in shape." He started to say something else when he suddenly stopped. He was looking at something over Susan's shoulder. Susan half turned around to see a tall, attractive woman accompanied by a teenage girl.

"Hello, Brian," the woman said, stopping at their table. She looked curiously at Susan. The teenager, a pretty redhead, also looked at Susan.

"Hello, Priscilla. Hi, Brittany. Um, this is Susan Pickering. Susan, I'd like you to meet Priscilla Dunn and her daughter Brittany."

"Nice to meet you," the Dunn woman said.

"Thank you. You, too." But Susan sensed more than curiosity in the woman's gaze, and it made her uncomfortable.

There was an awkward moment after that when no one said anything. Then the Dunn woman said, "Well, we won't keep you. Nice to see you, Brian." She flicked another glance Susan's way. A few moments later, they were being seated across the room.

Susan didn't look, but she knew Priscilla Dunn was looking at them. That was one of the hazards of living in a small town. Your business didn't stay your business for very long. Tomorrow—maybe even tonight—quite a few people would know that Susan Pickering had been seen having dinner with Brian Murphy.

Susan didn't mind. But from the expression on his face, she knew Brian did.

As they finished their dinner and he paid the check and collected his pizza, Susan told herself she didn't care that she probably wouldn't be hearing from Brian again.

But she knew she *did* care.

She cared a lot.

Chapter Four

Brian knew that it would only be a matter of hours before Kaycee and Janna discovered he'd taken Susan out to dinner, so he decided he'd better say something to the girls before Priscilla Dunn had a chance to make the evening sound other than what it was.

Janna was sitting on the porch swing when he pulled in front of the house at eight o'clock. Jumping off, she bounded down the steps to meet him. "Oh, good, you're early," she said, giving him a hug. "I'm starved."

Brian chuckled. Janna was always starved. "Where's your sister?"

Janna made a face. "On the phone, where else?"

Together they walked into the house. As always it

gave him a pang to enter as a guest instead of as someone who belonged there. He fought the feeling, knowing it was counterproductive, but sometimes he wasn't successful.

"Pizza's here, Kaycee," Brian called upstairs on his way back to the kitchen.

"Okay," she shouted down. "I'm coming." A few minutes later she walked into the kitchen. She, too, hugged him.

She's in a good mood tonight, he thought thankfully. With Kaycee, you never knew. She was in the throes of teenage angst, and some days she was barely tolerable. Tonight she looked happy, as if it had been a good day. Her blond hair, the same shade Lonnie's had been as a kid, hung in wet ringlets; it was obvious she'd washed it earlier. Her blue eyes, a mirror image of his own, were shining. Brian could never look at her or Janna without a warm feeling of pride. They were both good kids: beautiful and smart and mostly loving. What more could any parent ask for?

Once the girls were settled at the table, scarfing down their pizza, Brian poured himself a cold glass of water and sat down with them.

"Guess who I saw tonight," he said to Kaycee.

"Who?" she said around a mouthful of pizza.

"Brittany."

"Oh, yeah? Where?"

"At Tony's. She was with her mom."

"Yeah, she said she was going there tonight." She

polished off her first piece of pizza and reached for a second. "Were you there by yourself?"

The question was asked so casually, Brian knew there was nothing behind it except normal curiosity. "No, I was there with a woman whose case I'm investigating."

"What kind of case?" Janna asked eagerly, her own blue eyes alight.

Brian smiled. Janna had ideas about joining the police force when she grew up. Brian wasn't sure he wanted her to, yet he couldn't help feeling proud that she admired what he did enough to want to do it herself. "You know I'm not supposed to discuss my cases."

"Oh, Dad. As long as you don't name names..." She gave him one of her wheedling grins.

Brian guessed there would be no harm done if he just stuck to generalities. "Someone charged thousands of dollars on this woman's credit card, and I'm doing some investigating from this end."

"Identity theft," Janna pronounced with relish. "I read about it on the Internet."

"Well, we don't know if it's identity theft or not. So far it's just the one credit card that seems to have been used."

"What'll happen when you find the person who did it?" she asked.

"That depends."

"Jeez, Janna, why do you *care*, anyway?" Kaycee said, rolling her eyes.

Brian stifled a grin at the look of disgust on his older daughter's face. Kaycee made no secret of the fact she considered her sister a goober. Not that she used words like *goober.* She was too cool for that. Janna, on the other hand, thought Kaycee was stupid.

"All she cares about is boys and clothes and makeup, Dad," Janna had complained one day. "Doesn't she know there are more important things to think about, like how crowded our prisons are? Like how we're losing the war on drugs? Like how our police officers and firefighters and teachers don't get paid enough?"

Sometimes Janna scared Brian. How could a not-quite-thirteen-year-old be so mature about so many things? He also wondered how it was possible for the same two people to have two children so radically different. Kaycee, the girly girl, and Janna, out to save the world. *You and Kevin were completely different, too, don't forget....*

Brian pushed that thought away. He didn't like thinking about Kevin, because when he did, he felt guilty. He'd known his brother was experimenting with drugs; he'd even warned him about how danger-ous drugs were, especially cocaine, but Kevin had insisted he could handle it. "I only do a little at par-ties," he'd said with one of those disarming grins of his. "No big deal."

Brian shouldn't have listened. He should have followed his instincts and told his parents. But he was young, barely twenty, and he hadn't wanted to squeal on his brother.

If only I had, maybe things would have turned out differently. Maybe Kevin wouldn't have died. Maybe Mom's and Dad's hearts wouldn't have been broken.

"Hey, Dad," Kaycee was saying, "You wouldn't like to contribute to my school clothes fund, would you?"

"What school clothes fund?" Brian said, playing dumb.

Kaycee gave him a look. "You know I need new clothes for school this year."

"I thought that's where your summer babysitting money was going."

"It *is,* but it's not enough, and Mom says she can only afford to give me a hundred dollars more to add to it."

"So what'll be your total then?"

"Five hundred," she mumbled.

"Kaycee, I would think five hundred dollars is plenty for new school clothes."

"Daaaad…"

"Look, Kaycee, I can't afford to pay for hundred-dollar designer jeans. And even if I could, I wouldn't, because I don't believe in buying clothes that expensive unless it's a winter coat or something. Five hundred dollars is *plenty* for new school clothes. Besides, your birthday's next week. And you know your Sherman grandparents always give you money." He pushed the thought of Ed Grayling and his offer out of his mind. It wasn't relevant to this situation.

Kaycee looked as if she wanted to argue, but she didn't, and Brian was glad. He hated saying no to either of his girls—a hazard of being a divorced parent—but Kaycee's champagne tastes needed toning down.

Ah, hell, maybe I should have just given her money for her birthday, too, let her buy whatever she wanted with it.

But he wasn't sorry he'd bought the brooch. It would be something special she'd have for a long time, whereas clothes—especially the stuff she liked—quickly went out of style and were long forgotten.

Getting up, he carried his empty glass to the dishwasher and put it in. "I've got to go. You guys going to be okay till your mom gets home?"

The words were barely out of his mouth when he heard the key in the back door. A minute later Lonnie walked into the kitchen. Her smile was friendly as her green eyes met his. "Hello, Brian."

"Hi, Lonnie. I was just leaving."

"You don't have to leave on my account."

"I know. But I've got some stuff I need to do before I can call it a night."

He kissed both girls goodbye, saying, "I'll see you Tuesday night."

"Six o'clock," Lonnie said.

"Okay. Is everyone coming? My sisters?"

"Everyone but Caitlin. She'll be out of town on business."

"Darn," Kaycee said. "I hardly ever get to see Aunt Caitlin."

Caitlin was an account rep for a big Columbus-based advertising agency and traveled a lot to client sites.

"She said to tell you she was sending your gift with Aunt Brenda," Lonnie said.

Brian smiled ruefully. Lonnie talked to Caitlin— for that matter, *all* his sisters—more often than he did. "Okay, well, I really have to go."

"'Bye, Dad," said the girls.

"Good night, Brian," said Lonnie. She gave him another smile.

As Brian walked down the driveway toward his car, he thought about how much easier life would be if he loved Lonnie and they were still married. If that were the case, he wouldn't have had to leave the home they'd struggled to buy and had lived in with such pride. He'd have changed clothes and headed toward the room they'd made into a study for him. He'd have been there to kiss the girls good-night when they went upstairs to bed, and he and Lonnie would have companionably watched the late news together, maybe over a glass of wine, before heading off to bed themselves.

Instead, he was on his way to his small apartment where his only company would be the TV set.

And yet Brian had no regrets about the divorce. He had married Lonnie because they were friends and because everyone expected him to, but there'd never been any passion in the relationship, at least not on his part, and he'd finally had to admit it.

He'd stuck it out a long time, but staying married to her when he didn't love her wasn't fair to either of them. He had wanted to love her. Yet as hard as he tried, he couldn't change the way he felt.

He'd kept wishing she'd confront him. But she never did, and he figured he knew why. She was afraid of what he'd say. So, although it was hard, he finally told her they needed to talk. He took all the blame. He told her he knew she was unhappy and he understood why.

"I'm not good husband material," he'd said.

"Do you think we should split up?" she'd finally asked.

"Don't you?" he'd countered.

He was relieved when she said yes. And in the end, he knew she was better off. Now she might find someone else, someone who could love her the way she deserved to be loved.

He hoped so.

He wanted only the best for Lonnie.

And then, unbidden, the image of Susan as she'd looked sitting across the table from him tonight filled his mind. He knew it was foolish to think about her in any way other than as a victim of a crime he was investigating.

But try as he might, he couldn't rid himself of the thought that if only he'd met her a year or two from now, when he was in a better position to get involved in a relationship, she might have turned out to be *his* someone else.

Susan thought about calling Ann when she got home, but for some reason she hesitated. *I'm just not ready to talk about my feelings for Brian.*

What exactly *were* her feelings for him?

Susan wasn't sure. She only knew being with him made her feel warm and safe. This surprised her, for she hadn't realized she *didn't* feel safe. After all, she'd been on her own for a long time. She'd held a responsible job, then she'd raised her sister all on her own, and for the past eight years she'd run a successful business.

Still, if she were being completely honest with herself, she'd admit how many times she'd wished she had some family to count on. Someone to help out when the going got rough. Even an older brother or sister would have been great, but there was nobody, only Sasha.

Sasha.

While they'd been at the restaurant, Susan had hardly thought about Sasha. Now, though, the full import of the information Brian had given her sank in.

Where *was* Sasha? And who was the "loser" she was with? More important, when would Susan hear from her again?

Please God, let me be right. Let it be one of her

worthless friends who's behind the charges on my credit card.

Because if it turned out to be Sasha, as Brian obviously thought, Susan wasn't sure she could handle it.

"Happy birthday to you, happy birthday to you, happy birthday, dear Kayceeeee. Happy birthday to you."

Brian smiled as he watched his newly turned fifteen-year-old blow out her candles. He was determined not to let the awkwardness of being in the company of Lonnie's parents detract from Kaycee's birthday party.

Lou and Ginny Sherman still hadn't forgiven him for divorcing their daughter. Brian wasn't sure they ever would. Their attitude had made it tough on Brian's parents, too, because the Shermans and the Murphys had been neighbors and best friends for as long as Brian could remember.

You'd think, after three years, they'd have accepted that Lonnie and Brian had moved on, but things were still strained when the families met for celebrations like these.

"Can I open my presents now?" Kaycee said once everyone had been served cake.

"Yes, you *may,*" Lonnie said.

"Oh, Mom." Kaycee reached for a large box Brian knew had come from Caitlin. She squealed when she lifted out first a white blouse, then a blue tweed jacket with some kind of fringe on the sleeves and bottom. "Oh, *I love it*!" She jumped up, holding the jacket up against her. "Oh, it's perfect! I can't wait to wear it! I'm so glad it's not hot anymore. I'll wear it tomorrow night."

"What's tomorrow night?" Brian's sister Brenda asked.

"A CYO mixer," Kaycee said.

Brian looked at Lonnie, who winked. He remembered when Kaycee would rather have been struck dumb than have to attend anything connected with CYO—the Catholic Youth Organization—at St. Helen's, the church where his and Lonnie's families had belonged all of their lives. But Lonnie had told Brian not long ago that a boy Kaycee currently had a crush on was the vice president of the group and now nothing would keep her from the meetings and activities.

Love definitely made the world go round, Brian thought ruefully. Even Janna would succumb someday.

Kaycee continued to open presents and, as Brian had predicted, her Sherman grandparents had given her a generous check. So had his parents.

Janna had even come around, giving Kaycee a subscription to *Seventeen* magazine. She'd originally wanted to make a donation to World Relief in Kaycee's name, but Brian had talked her out of it, saying he'd send a donation in both the girls' names and to just buy Kaycee a normal present.

"Birthdays aren't days to make statements," he said gently, "or to show disapproval of your sister."

"Oh, okay, Dad," Janna said.

Kaycee opened Brian's present close to the end. Her mouth dropped open when she saw the brooch. "Daddy! It's *gorgeous*. I love it! And it'll look *awesome* on my new jacket." She jumped up and came over to him, giving him a big hug.

Brian smiled. "Glad you like it, honey."

Lonnie gave him a speculative look. He knew she wondered how he'd ever known brooches were so popular with teenage girls.

Just then his mother touched his arm, saying, "Hasn't Lonnie put on a nice party?"

"She has," Brian agreed.

"Of course, she always does."

"Yes, she does." He braced himself, knowing what would inevitably come.

"She's a wonderful mother."

Brian didn't say anything.

"Well, she *is*."

"Yes, she's a wonderful mother. I never said she wasn't."

"You know, Brian, it's not too late for you two—"

"Mom." He cut her off in midsentence. Lowering his voice, he said, "Stop, okay? It's over." It was bad enough Lonnie's parents couldn't adjust to reality. Why couldn't his *own* parents give it a rest?

Seeing the hurt look on his mother's face, he immediately felt bad. She loved him, and she meant well. *Dammit*. "I'm sorry," he said softly.

"I just want you to be happy."

"I know." But that wasn't all she wanted, and they both knew it. She wanted him and Lonnie to get back together. That would make *her* happy.

Thankfully, the party now began to break up, with his sister Brenda starting to gather up her three, and Lonnie's sister Linda following suit with her two.

Brian stood, uncertain as to whether to hang around or beat a quick exit. He knew Kaycee would want him to stay longer. She, of course, was as bad as his mother. She'd said only last week how she wished he'd come back home. He sighed. Why did divorce have to be so hard on everyone? Thank goodness Lonnie seemed to be okay. If he'd had to see miserable looks from her, too, he wasn't sure he could stand it.

"You going to stay awhile, Brian?" Lonnie said, moving over to his side.

"Sure."

She smiled at him. "Good. Kaycee would be disappointed if you left."

Sometimes he wondered if Lonnie still loved him. He hoped not. It was hard to tell because, except for the few days after he'd told her he wanted a divorce, she had seemed to bounce right back to her positive, upbeat attitude. During their marriage, that attitude had sometimes gotten on his nerves, especially in their latter years together. He'd finally said, "Lonnie, not everyone is nice. Not everyone has your best interest at heart. Not everything is going to turn out well. Get real, for crying out loud." Then he'd felt guilty for hurting her feelings and raining on her parade. But mostly he'd felt guilty for not loving her.

He wondered now if Lonnie had been dating at all since the divorce. He didn't think she had because surely the girls would have said something? Well, it wasn't that easy to reenter the dating scene, as he should know, he thought ruefully.

It took another thirty minutes before everyone but Brian had gone. There was only one awkward moment toward the end when Ginny Sherman, saying a cool goodbye, stiffened as he bent to kiss her cheek. It saddened Brian. He'd always liked Ginny. Lou was a bit of a blowhard, but still, they were both good people. He was sorry he'd had to hurt them. He couldn't imagine what family gatherings would be like if he ever married again.

"So," Lonnie said sotto voce when she shut the door after the last guest, "how'd you ever think to give Kaycee that beautiful brooch?"

"There's a case I'm working on involving a woman who owns that antique shop in the Mill Creek Center. Anyway, when I was in the shop to talk to her last week, I happened to see the jewelry she handles. She suggested the brooch. Said all the girls are wearing them nowadays."

"Well, it's beautiful. It was an inspired gift. Kaycee loves it." She let it drop.

After that, Brian and the girls helped Lonnie clean up, then the four of them sat around the kitchen table—Lonnie and Brian over cups of coffee, the girls with soft drinks. Brian stayed until ten-thirty, then finally got up to leave.

Lonnie walked him to the front door. Just as he was about to walk out, she said, "Brian, I'm sorry about the way my parents acted tonight."

He shrugged. "They can't help how they feel."

"The thing is, I've told them over and over that there are no hard feelings between you and me and that their attitude is just making it tougher on all of us."

"Well, in some ways, they're justified in how they feel. They think I treated you badly." He swallowed. "I'm really sorry if I hurt you, Lonnie. You know that, don't you?"

"Of course I know that. You can't help how *you* feel, either." Then she smiled. "Anyway, I'm over it. I realize we're both better off now."

"You're not just saying that?"

She shook her head. "Trust me. I'm not. I really mean it."

Brian looked down into her eyes for a long moment. What he saw there reassured him. She *did* mean it. "Some guy is going to get really lucky one of these days when he finds you."

She chuckled. "Oh, can that Irish blarney and go home."

Brian was still smiling ten minutes later.

For the first time in a long time, all five members of the Wednesday-night gang were meeting for dinner. No one was sick; no one was away on business; no one was on vacation.

"Zoe, it's *so* good to see you!" Susan said, giving the new Mrs. Sam Welch a hug. "How was the honeymoon?"

Zoe, a vibrant redhead, smiled wickedly. "Everything a honeymoon *should* be."

Ann sighed. "I'm so jealous. Not only does she find a handsome, eligible man, but he's *rich*, too."

Ann's sister Carol winked at Zoe. "Don't mind her. She's fixated on money."

"I am *not*!" Ann said, smacking Carol's arm. "Am I, Susan?"

Susan held up her hands. "Don't get me in the middle of a family argument."

"You're supposed to be my friend," Ann grumbled, but she was laughing.

"Settle down, girls," Shawn said. "People are beginning to look at us."

"The reason they look at us," Ann retorted, "is because we're all so gorgeous."

"You *wish*," Carol cracked.

Zoe shook her head. "You guys never change." Then she grinned. "Thank God."

After that they did settle down, and listened avidly as Zoe described her trip. She'd been gone the entire summer. First she'd gone to England with her daughter, Emma, new wife of Kirby Gates, the rhythm guitar player in the famous rock band Freight Train, where Zoe got to meet Emma's new in-laws. From there Zoe had traveled along with the band, which Emma was now a part of. Sam Welch, who managed the band for his half brother Zach Trainer—who just happened to be Emma's father—was with them, too. He and Zoe were married in Paris, which was the band's last tour stop in Europe, and from there, they'd traveled to Australia and New Zealand for their honeymoon. Now both Sam and Zoe were back to work. Zoe said that soon Sam was moving his headquarters from Los Angeles to Columbus so they wouldn't have to be apart so much.

"What about that beach house he bought?" Shawn asked. "Is he selling that?"

"No," Zoe said. "It's going to be our retirement home, and in the meantime, we'll spend as much time there as we can manage."

"Jeez, Zoe," Ann said, "if I were married to Sam Welch, I'd quit my job and live wherever he wanted to live."

"I *like* my job, Ann," Zoe said.

Zoe was the manager of Berry's, one of Columbus's top department stores.

"Getting married in Paris, traveling with the band, honeymooning in Australia and New Zealand—it all sounds so incredibly romantic, Zoe," Shawn said.

Susan agreed. She couldn't imagine taking such a trip, and to take it with the man you loved, well, it would be any woman's dream. "If anyone deserves this, you do, Zoe," she said.

"Thanks, Susan, but I don't think I'm any more deserving than any one of you," Zoe said. "Now I want to hear what's been happening here while I was gone. Besides Shawn having her baby." She grinned at Shawn. "Which we all agree is the most beautiful child ever born."

Shawn laughed.

"I've been dating one of the engineers at our firm," Carol said.

"Really, Carol?" This came from Shawn. "Tell us about him."

"Well, he's really sweet. Kind of shy, but nice. And he *loves* to hike."

"He sounds perfect for you," Zoe said.

"I know," Carol said with a grimace, "and I keep wondering what his fatal flaw will turn out to be."

After that the talk turned to Susan, who had to explain to Zoe all about her problems with her Visa credit card.

"And," Ann said when Susan had finished, "Susan's leaving out the best part. She's dating the cop who's on her case."

"Ann," Susan protested, "I'm not *dating* him. I just had dinner with him, and that was probably because he felt sorry for me." Turning to Zoe, she added, "He'd just told me that Sasha had taken off for parts unknown." She tried to keep her voice nonchalant, but she knew she wasn't kidding anyone. All of her friends understood how much it hurt her when Sasha pulled one of her stunts.

"Brian Murphy seems like a really nice man," Shawn said. "I know his sister thinks the world of him."

"That's right," Susan said. "You're friends with one of his sisters, aren't you?" She wanted to ask what Caitlin was like, but she didn't want her friends to know just how much she liked Brian.

"*One* of his sisters?" Ann teased. "Looks like you know a whole lot more about the sexy cop than you're letting on."

"We had to talk about *something* during dinner," Susan said, "so we talked about our families."

After that the subject of Brian was dropped, but Susan continued to think about him. She hadn't heard from him since that dinner together. Five days. If he really liked her, wouldn't he have called her by now?

All you are is a case to him. The only reason he

took you to dinner on Friday was because he felt sorry for you.

Face it, Susan, she told herself, he's not going to call you. So if you're smart, you'll put him out of your mind.

Chapter Five

"So...have you heard from the sexy cop yet?" Ann asked.

Susan was glad they were chatting on the phone, because she knew the disappointment she felt probably showed on her face. "Nope, but I didn't expect to. I told you. Friday night wasn't a date."

"Oh, c'mon. A good-looking guy asks you out to dinner and *pays*...he *did* pay, didn't he?"

"Yes." Susan had tried to pay her share, but Brian wouldn't let her.

"Well then, I consider that a date."

Susan had hoped it was a date. Just as she'd hoped to hear from Brian by now. Tomorrow it would be a week. *I'm not going to hear from him until he has news for me. He considers me a case, that's all.*

"Why don't you call him?"

"Because I don't want to."

"Why not?"

"Ann! I am not, repeat, *not* going to chase after someone who isn't interested in me."

"Just call him and ask him if he's had any news about Sasha."

"He'd call me if he had any news."

"Well, duh. I know that, and you know that, but he doesn't have to *know* that you know that. Play dumb, Susan. Use your feminine wiles."

Susan shook her head. "He knows I'm not dumb."

"C'mon, Susan, work with me here. Just pretend to be dumb about police procedure. Would that kill you?"

"What's the point? He'll just say he hasn't heard anything, and then I'll feel stupid and then he'll make an excuse to get off the phone. It's too demoralizing. I'm not calling him."

Ann's sigh was loud. "We'll talk about this more in depth when I see you. Which reminds me. We still on for a movie Sunday afternoon?"

"Sure."

"Want to grab a bite afterward?

"Sounds good."

"By the way, how's your customer-appreciation sale going?"

Susan smiled. The sale was the one bright spot of

the week. She might not have heard from Sasha, and she might not have heard from Brian, but she was selling tons of stuff. "Even better than I'd hoped."

"That's terrific. Maybe now you can do that online store."

"I'd like to, but we'll have to see."

"Well, if you decide to do it, I know a gal who is a whiz at designing Web sites, and she's reasonable. Hey, that reminds me. Later today I'll drop off a check for that creamer and sugar bowl set I bought."

"There's no hurry."

"I know, but I don't want to forget about it. Besides, you know me." She chuckled. "Money tends to burn a hole in my pocket. If I don't pay you, I might be tempted to spend it."

Out of the corner of her eye, Susan saw the shadow of someone outside the shop door. She turned to see who was entering, and her heart stuttered in her chest. It was Brian. "Um, Ann, listen, I have to go. I've got a customer."

"Okay, see you later."

Susan hung up and tried to make her smile casual, although her body was humming with excitement.

"Hi, Susan." His smile was warm.

"Hi."

"Don't get your hopes up. I don't have any news."

"I wasn't really expecting any."

"I just stopped in to tell you there's not much

more I can do on your case. It's now in the hands of the credit card company."

Susan couldn't help the sudden pang of disappointment, because she knew if he was off the case she was unlikely to see Brian again. Her eyes met his, and she hoped they didn't reflect her thoughts. "That's okay. I pretty much figured that out."

He hesitated. "But I'll be glad to help you in any way I can—not officially, of course—but as a friend."

Susan smiled. "That's awfully nice of you, but you don't have to do that."

"I know, but I want to."

Something about the way he was looking at her made Susan feel he really meant what he was saying, and hope flared again. "Well, thank you, then."

"I don't suppose you've heard from your sister?"

Susan sighed. "No."

He nodded thoughtfully. "If you do, will you let me know?"

Now it was Susan's turn to hesitate. *Would she?* "Yes, I will," she finally said. Then, because she didn't want to discuss Sasha anymore, she said, "On a more upbeat subject, how'd your daughter like the brooch you gave her?"

He grinned. "She loved it. Said it was awesome."

"I'm so glad."

For a moment silence settled between them. Susan racked her brain trying to think of something innocuous to talk about, but she could think of nothing but a comment on the weather, which was warm again, and how dumb was *that*?

Oh, why couldn't she have Zoe's biting wit or Ann's ability to make small talk? Why did she have to feel like a tongue-tied teenager in the company of the school's star quarterback?

"Susan…" he began.

"I, um…" she said.

Then they both laughed.

"What were you going to say?" he asked.

"Nothing important. What were *you* going to say?"

"I was, uh, wondering if you might like to catch a movie Saturday night?"

Susan hoped her smile didn't reveal the sheer joy that had zinged through her at his question. "I'd love to. Which movie did you have in mind?"

"There's a new thriller with Denzel Washington that looks good."

"That sounds perfect." Susan was glad he hadn't picked the movie she'd promised to see with Ann on Sunday.

"Afterward maybe we can grab a hamburger or something."

"Okay."

"What time do you close the shop on Saturdays?"

"Not till six."

"Why don't I check the movie schedule and give you a call, then we can decide on a time."

Susan knew she was grinning like a fool after he'd

gone. She wanted to call Ann right away and tell her what had happened, but she had a string of customers after Brian left. Thursday was her late night, and she always got people on their way home from work. Tonight was no different.

About six o'clock an attractive woman with honey-blond hair walked in. Susan was good at remembering faces, and she knew immediately this woman had never been in the shop before. "Hello," she said, giving her a welcoming smile. "May I help you?"

The woman smiled back. "If you don't mind, I'd just like to browse around for a while."

"I don't mind at all. Just let me know if you have any questions."

"Thank you. I will."

Susan busied herself at the front counter and after about ten minutes, the woman walked back to the front. "You have some lovely things here," she said.

"Thank you."

The woman approached the counter and gazed down into the glass case at the jewelry display. "Oh," she said. "Those earrings. May I see them?" She pointed to a set of amethyst drops.

"Of course." Susan unlocked the display case and took them out, laying them on top of the counter for the woman to take a closer look.

The woman held them up to her ears and looked at herself in the little mirror Susan had for that purpose. "They're so beautiful."

"They look nice on you, too." The woman's eyes were a soft shade of green.

"How much are they?" she asked.

"They're sixty dollars, but if you want them, I'll give them to you for forty-eight."

The woman bit her lip. "I really shouldn't, but what the heck, my birthday's coming up later this month." She grinned. "I'll give myself a birthday present."

"Good for you." Susan reached into the case again. Taking out the bracelet that matched the earrings, she said, "You might hint to your husband or parents that you'd like to have this bracelet, too."

"Ohh," the woman said. "It's gorgeous. Maybe I'll tell my mother about it. She always buys me something nice, so why not this?"

"Do you want me to put it aside so that no one else will buy it?"

"*Would* you?"

"Of course."

"Her name is Ginny Sherman."

"Okay, great. Consider it done. Now how did you want to pay for the earrings?"

"I'll just write you a check." The woman dug in her handbag and pulled out a combination wallet and checkbook.

Susan rang up the sale and told the woman the amount. The woman wrote the check and handed it to Susan. Susan was about to ask to see a driver's license when she noticed the name—L. N. Murphy. Susan wondered if she was related to Brian's family.

"You know," the Murphy woman said, "my daughter got a beautiful brooch for her birthday from her dad, and he said it came from here."

Ohmigod, Susan thought. *This is Brian's ex-wife.* For a moment she was flustered, but she quickly regained her poise. "Your daughter's name is Kaycee, isn't it?" She asked as she wrapped the earrings in tissue and put them in a small bag.

Lonnie Murphy smiled. "You remembered."

"It wasn't hard. I've only sold one brooch in the past month. And your, um—"

"My ex-husband," Lonnie supplied.

"Your ex-husband said it was for your oldest daughter."

"She loved it, too. In fact, she's worn it practically every day since. Her aunt gave her a darling little blue tweed jacket that looks so cute with jeans, and that brooch is perfect for it." Lonnie grinned. "Of course, this week it's too warm to wear the jacket, but Kaycee doesn't care as long as she looks good."

Susan grinned, thinking of Ann. "I've got a friend like that." Lonnie seemed really nice, but Susan couldn't help but wonder if she'd come into the shop to check Susan out. It seemed far-fetched. After all, how would she know that Susan was dating Brian, because now that he'd asked her to go to the movies, Susan guessed they *were* dating. Then Susan remembered the woman—she thought her name was Prudence or Priscilla or something like that—they'd seen at Tony's last Friday night. Hadn't Brian said she was Lonnie's best friend? Or had she imagined that? Maybe he'd said the daughter was his daughter's friend?

Remembering, Susan felt awkward. Of course Lonnie had come in to check Susan out. In her shoes, Susan would have done the same thing. She wondered if Lonnie was still in love with Brian.

"Well," Lonnie Murphy said, "thanks for your help. I'll be sure and tell my mother about the bracelet." Her smile seemed genuine and warm.

Susan decided Lonnie was either the best actress in the world or she genuinely wasn't bothered by the fact Brian was dating someone. It was hard for Susan to believe it was the latter. Wouldn't it be normal for Brian's ex-wife to be bothered by his dating? Especially when, if Susan had understood the situation correctly, Brian was the one who'd wanted the divorce?

What if Lonnie had only pretended to be checking out the shop when she was really checking out Susan so she could decide what to do about her? What if she decided to undermine Susan by talking about her to the girls?

What have you gotten yourself into, Susan? Are you really sure you want to get involved with someone like Brian? Doesn't he come with a bit too much baggage?

Of course, Susan thought ruefully, she had some baggage of her own.

Susan's pleasure over Brian's invitation to the movies faded. She was afraid she was kidding herself. Her relationship with Brian Murphy didn't seem promising. If she had any sense at all, she'd call him right now and tell him she'd changed her mind about Saturday night.

The twin aromas of cabbage and corned beef greeted Brian and the girls when they walked into his parents' house. Brian grinned. His mother never let him down. At least once a month she made his favorite meal.

"Hello, my darlings," his mother said, walking out to the foyer to greet them.

"Hi, Gran," they said in unison.

Brian's mother wiped her hands on her ever-present apron, then hugged the girls. She then presented her cheek for Brian to kiss.

"Where's Grandpa?" Janna asked.

"Out back in the garden."

The garden was his father's great passion. Every summer he grew wonderful tomatoes, radishes, lettuce, onions, zucchini, cucumbers, green beans, yellow squash and corn. He also had a strawberry patch and two cherry trees, all of which yielded enough fruit to supply the entire family, plus a few neighbors.

"Let's go see him," Janna said, heading for the back of the house. Kaycee followed more slowly.

"He must be feeling good today," Brian commented as he and his mother walked to the kitchen.

"Yes, it's a good day."

In the kitchen his mother stopped at the stove where she lifted the lid on the big pot she always used for her corned beef and cabbage. As she stirred, her back to him, Brian studied his mother's trim figure. As far as he could tell, she hadn't gained a pound since he was a boy. It was amazing, too, considering the way she cooked, which also hadn't changed since he was young. Other families had had to adjust their diets to cut down on fat or sugar, but the Murphys still ate as if there were no tomorrow.

"Do you want something to drink?" his mother asked, putting the lid back on her pot.

"I'll get it." Brian opened the refrigerator and took out a bottle of Guinness.

"Go say hello to your father, then come back and talk to me," his mother said.

Brian found his father showing the girls the last of his summer tomatoes. His hands shook from the Parkinson's as he picked one and handed it to Janna. Watching the three of them together, Brian got one of those lumps in his throat that seemed to come more often lately when he was around his father. Michael Murphy, called Mickey by almost everyone, was seventy-two—not old considering how long seniors seemed to live today—yet Brian was acutely aware of the fact his parents wouldn't live forever.

His father's brother, Patrick, who'd gone back to Ireland ten years earlier, had died six months ago at the age of seventy-five. And his sister, Maureen, had died last year at the age of seventy-seven.

Brian didn't like thinking about losing his parents. So mostly he didn't. Except on days like today, when for some reason, he felt more vulnerable to the inevitability of their eventual deaths.

"Hello, Brian," his father said, pronouncing the word *hallow* instead of *hello*. "These lasses of yours are giving me some lip today."

"Oh, Grandpa, we are not," Janna said, laughing.

Kaycee grinned. "Grandpa said the most beautiful women come from Ireland."

"And all we said was," Janna put in, "that Mom isn't Irish and *she's* beautiful."

"Well, me girls, there are some exceptions, to be sure, and your mother is one of them, but by and large, what I said is true. And you two are perfect examples of fine Irish beauty."

"Only half Irish, Grandpa," Janna said.

"Such a stickler for the absolute truth," Brian's father said, his blue eyes twinkling.

Brian chuckled. His father was in fine form today.

"Brian, me boy, would you like to take these tomatoes in to your mother?"

Brian took the tomatoes from his father and went back into the house. He was glad to see the girls were content to stay outdoors with his dad. That was one thing he'd say about the girls—they never seemed to mind being with their grandparents. Just the opposite, in fact. Brian knew he was fortunate. He'd heard the tales some of his friends told about practically having to drag their kids to see their parents. Well, maybe it was more than luck involved. Both he and Lonnie had always stressed the importance of family, and the girls obviously felt the same way.

"Thank you," his mother said when he gave her the tomatoes. "Now, sit down. Let's talk."

Brian wondered what his mother had on her mind. He didn't have long to wait. Pulling a chair out across from him, she sat down. Her blue eyes met his.

"What?" he said, frowning.

"Cynthia Prescott tells me you're dating."

Brian knew there was no reason for him to feel guilty, yet his heart knocked at her words. "That's what I hate about living in a small town," he said, not even trying to disguise the fact he was angry. "There's no privacy and there's no lack of busybodies."

"Cynthia Prescott is a lovely woman and she is *not* a busybody."

"Yeah? Obviously she couldn't wait to tell you something that is none of her business. I'm surprised you didn't say something in front of everyone at Kaycee's birthday party."

His mother's gaze hardened. "I didn't know about it then, but even if I did, I would never have said anything in front of Lonnie."

"I'm sure Lonnie knows."

"You didn't *tell* her, I hope."

"Now why would I do that?"

"I don't know, Brian. I don't know why you do a lot of things."

Brian got up. He was sick and tired of being the bad guy when he was just a normal man who got a divorce, just like millions of other men. "Look, Mom, I don't want to fight with you. But I don't need this. Tell the girls I was paged and had to go."

His mother stared at him. "Don't act like a child, Brian. Sit down."

"Quit treating me like a child, then."

"I just asked you a simple question."

"No, you didn't. You said Cynthia Prescott told you I was dating."

"Well? *Are* you?"

Brian gritted his teeth. "I've dated a few women over the past three years, yes."

"And you're dating someone now?"

"Yes."

His mother sighed. "Oh, Brian. You're such a fool. Lonnie is such a wonderful—"

"Stop it, Mom. Stop it right now. Lonnie and me, we're history. I don't love her. I've told you that a dozen times. Our marriage—it wasn't good for either one of us. She deserves better. And so do I."

"But—"

"No buts about it. And I'll tell you, if you don't

stop harping about Lonnie, I'm going to stop coming over here. I love you and I love Pop, but I don't need this. And frankly, neither does she."

For a long moment the only sounds were the muted laughter outside, the loud ticking of the wall clock and the soft hum of the refrigerator. Finally she sighed. "I'm sorry."

"Are you?"

She looked up. "Yes, I am."

"Okay. I accept your apology."

"But I'd still like to know about this woman you're seeing."

"When I think there's anything to tell you, I will. Until then, I prefer not to talk about her."

To his mother's credit, she just nodded. Then she got up and walked to the stove. A moment later she carried a pot to the sink and drained off the water. Brian knew there were potatoes inside and she would soon busy herself mashing them. He finished his Guinness in one long swallow, then got up and walked over to her. Putting his arm around her, he rested his head against hers.

"Love you, Mom," he said softly.

She glanced up. "I love you, too, Brian."

"Even when I do things you don't approve of?"

She smiled. "Even then."

Chapter Six

"What do you *mean,* you're going to call him and tell him you can't go?"

Susan winced at Ann's tone. "I told you. This is a go-nowhere situation, so why make it worse?"

"Susan, you are seriously paranoid. Give me one good reason why you think the relationship is going nowhere?"

Susan sighed deeply. She'd already explained her rationale and the reasons behind it to Ann. She didn't feel like repeating herself.

"You are not going to cancel. Do you hear me?"

"How could I *not* hear you? You're shouting." Susan held the phone away from her ear.

"Well, how *else* am I supposed to get your attention? I'm warning you, Susan. If you cancel, I won't speak to you for the rest of your life."

Susan couldn't help laughing. "You know you don't mean that."

"I do mean it. I want nothing to do with idiots."

"But, Ann, don't you see that if I go out with Brian, I'm just setting myself up to get hurt?"

"No, I do not. So what if he has an ex-wife and a couple of kids? He didn't try to hide it, now, did he? And you said yourself, the ex seems really nice. She wasn't ugly to you or anything. So what if she was checking you out? That doesn't mean she has evil intentions. It just means she's a normal, curious woman.

"Think about it, Susan. Wouldn't *you* be curious if you found out your ex was dating someone? Especially if that someone might someday impact your children's lives? Hell, I'd find a reason to come to the store, too.

"Give Brian a chance. Give *yourself* a chance. Brian might turn out to be the best thing that's ever happened to you."

"You do have a point, I guess."

"A point? I've got about *ten* valid points. Okay, enough. It's settled. You're going. Now let's talk about the *really* important thing—what you're going to wear."

Susan grinned.

Maybe the reason I called Ann was because I wanted her to talk me out of canceling, she thought after the two of them had hung up.

Because the truth was, Susan felt relieved by Ann's reaction. She didn't want to cancel her date with Brian. Ann was right. Susan needed to give Brian a chance. She needed to give the fledgling relationship a chance. Maybe it *wouldn't* work out.

But then again, maybe it would.

Susan tried on four different outfits Saturday night before settling on black cropped pants, a lightweight coral sweater, dangling coral earrings and black mules with wedge heels.

When she was ready, she looked at herself in the mirror. She thought she looked nice and not too dressed up. After all, it was just a movie and a hamburger afterward. Brian might even wear jeans.

She fluffed her hair one more time, then grabbed her black handbag and a black shawl in case it was cold in the theater, and headed downstairs. The grandfather clock that had originally been her grandmother's was just chiming seven-thirty when the doorbell rang. She smiled. Brian was right on time.

Her breath hitched in anticipation. Opening the door, she saw she'd guessed right, he *had* worn jeans. Jeans paired with a white shirt open at the neck and soft-looking brown boots.

He looked entirely too good. And way too sexy. When he smiled at her and trained those blue eyes on her, she felt a shimmer travel straight down to her toes.

"Ready?" He gave her an admiring glance.

"Yes. Let me just set the alarm."

Outside, the evening was mild. There was still a hint of summer left in the air, but Susan knew that very soon the evenings would be chilly. She didn't mind. Autumn was her favorite time of year. She especially looked forward to the leaves turning color. Maple Hills, with its thousands of maple trees, always looked amazing. People came from miles around to see the village in its autumn finery. In fact, more Maple Hills brides picked October for their weddings than any other month.

Once they were settled in his Bronco, Brian inserted a CD. Susan smiled when the music began; she recognized Asleep at the Wheel. "I'm not a big fan of country music, but this is one of my favorite CDs."

He smiled, obviously pleased. "Mine, too."

When "San Antonio Rose" played, they both sang along.

"You have a nice voice," Susan said, thinking how much they could use another tenor in the church choir.

"Thanks." He laughed. "When I was a kid, I dreamed of singing in a rock band."

"One of my friends actually *did* that."

"Really? Anyone I know?"

As he had just pulled into the shopping center where the theater was located, Susan said, "I'll tell you about her later. Remind me, okay?"

"Okay."

"Want some popcorn?" Brian asked when they were inside the theater.

"Movie popcorn is overpriced," Susan said, although she loved it and didn't think a movie was complete unless you had popcorn to eat while watching.

"Let's live dangerously."

"Only if you let me buy."

"No way. I invited you out, remember?"

"But you bought the tickets and you're taking me to get a hamburger later. It's only fair that I get the popcorn and drinks."

"Susan, call me old-fashioned, but I believe when a man invites a woman out, he pays for the entertainment."

Susan knew when to quit fighting a losing battle.

Later, settled three-quarters of the way up the theater's stadium-like seats, they companionably shared the large bag of popcorn and tolerated the too-loud commercials. "I hate these commercials," she said.

"Who doesn't?" he said.

"I love the previews, though."

"Yeah, most of the time they're better than the actual movie."

"You're a cynic, aren't you?" she said with a grin.

"Most cops are," he said wryly.

Susan was acutely aware of Brian sitting next to her, their arms touching as they shared the armrest between their seats. She loved the feeling of being part of a couple. Especially with a man as attractive and desirable as Brian.

Would they be a couple?

She thought he really liked her. And she certainly liked him. If only he didn't come with so much baggage. Unfortunately, as Ann had once pointed out, if a guy was near forty or older, and he was the kind of guy you could be interested in, he almost always came with baggage. For if he'd reached that age and had never been married, he was probably not the kind of guy you'd want.

Once the feature started, she stopped thinking about Brian and lost herself in the movie. When it was over, she sighed with satisfaction. She loved a happy ending, no matter what kind of story it was. Susan's friends loved to tease her about being a romantic, but she wasn't ashamed of it. There was nothing wrong in wanting things to work out well.

Leaving the theater, two women walked ahead of them. The older one reminded Susan of her mother, and for just a moment, a pang of sadness hit her. She quickly shook it off. She'd learned it didn't pay to dwell on what-might-have-beens.

They exited into the mall, and the women headed for the outside doors, but Brian said, "Do you mind? I want to go check out the phones." He inclined his head toward a telephone kiosk nearby. "I need a new one."

After a cursory look he said, "Let's go. I don't see anything I want."

The night air felt about ten degrees cooler as they walked outside, and Susan was glad of her shawl.

"Good movie, wasn't it?" Brian said, unlocking the door to the truck and helping her up.

"It was. I really like Denzel Washington."

"Yeah, he's a good actor. Some of the cop stuff was a little over the top, but other than that, I liked it."

He was about to close the passenger side door when a woman screamed nearby. "Help! Help! He took my purse!"

It was the older woman Susan had noticed earlier.

Brian took off like a shot in the direction the woman was pointing. Susan could see a man pounding across the parking lot with Brian in hot pursuit. Heart racing, Susan jumped out of the truck.

"Stop! Police!" Brian shouted.

The man kept running.

Susan whipped out her cell phone and dialed 911. She reported what had happened and that Brian was chasing the mugger, then she rushed over to the two women. The one whose purse had been taken was crying; the other was trying to comfort her, but her voice was trembling.

"Are you okay?" Susan asked.

"He took my purse," the older woman sobbed.

"Oh, Mary, it's okay," the younger woman said. Her eyes met Susan's.

"But it's not okay," the older woman cried. "My social security check's in there and my credit cards and my checkbook." She was shaking.

"Maybe your husband will catch him," the younger woman said to Susan.

"If anyone can, he can," Susan said. "He's a cop. I've also called for help." She hoped the help came soon. She could no longer see Brian, and it frightened her. She knew he didn't have a gun with him. What if something bad happened? What if the man who'd snatched Mary's purse *did* have a gun? She was also worried about the woman whose purse was stolen. She didn't look good to Susan. She wondered if she should call an ambulance.

While she was still trying to figure out what to do, a squad car pulled into the parking lot, and Susan waved him over. Thank God, she thought. When the uniformed officer got out of the car, the first thing he said was, "Where's Lieutenant Murphy?"

"He went that way," Susan said, pointing.

"Are you all right, ma'am?" the officer asked the older woman.

By now she'd calmed down a bit and she nodded. "Yes, but please find my purse."

Please find Brian, Susan thought.

The officer got back into the squad car and took off, siren going and lights flashing.

"Let's get your friend into your car," Susan suggested to the younger woman. "It'll be more comfortable there."

The next ten minutes seemed to crawl by, but

finally Susan saw the squad car coming back. *Please let Brian be there. Please let him be okay.*

Relief flooded her as the car pulled to stop and both Brian and the officer got out. She saw then that there was someone else in the backseat of the car.

Brian walked over to them. "Is this your purse, ma'am?" He handed it to the older woman, who had by now gotten out of the car.

"Oh, thank you, thank you," she said, a big smile wreathing her face.

He smiled back. "My pleasure. You might want to check it, make sure everything's there."

After riffling through its contents, she said, "Everything is here."

"That's good. I figured he didn't have time to take anything out." Turning to Susan, he said, "Do you mind if we go by the station before getting something to eat? I have to fill out a report."

"Of course not."

They sent the two women on their way, then followed the squad car to the police station.

"I'm so glad you were able to get that woman's purse back for her," Susan said.

"Yeah, me, too. But I'm even gladder I caught the kid who took it."

"I was frightened," Susan admitted.

He gave her a sidelong glance. "For me?"

"Yes. I knew you didn't have a weapon with you,

and I kept thinking, what if that guy had a gun? What if you were hurt?"

"Well, he didn't, and I wasn't."

"But you *could* have been. Weren't you taking a chance, going after him like that?"

Brian shrugged. "Susan, I'm a cop. I reacted like a cop. Sure, I was taking a chance, but I couldn't have done anything else. Not and lived with myself," he added. Then he smiled. "But thanks for worrying about me."

A minute later he pulled up in front of the police station. Susan went inside with him. It didn't take long—about thirty minutes—for Brian to type up his report and print it, and then they were once more on their way.

"I thought we might just go to Callie's. That okay with you?" Brian said.

"Callie's is one of my favorite places. In fact, I eat there every Wednesday night."

"No kidding?"

"Yes. I belong to this group of women. We call ourselves the Wednesday-night gang." Susan laughed. "Not very original, I know. Anyway, we get together for dinner every Wednesday. Have been doing so for years."

"That's great. You know, you women seem to be light-years ahead of us guys in the friendship department. I've got a couple of friends from school, and we play poker occasionally, but mostly I just hang out with other cops. When I'm not with my family, that is."

Susan nodded.

"You close to these women?"

"Yes. Very much so. In fact, they're pretty much like my family now. You met one of them last week at Tony's."

"Shawn McFarland, you mean?"

"Uh-huh."

"So what do you talk about on Wednesday nights?"

Susan grinned. "Everything."

"That means I'd better be on my good behavior tonight, right? Or you'll be telling stories about me."

Susan laughed.

A few minutes later he said, "You told me to remind you about the friend who sang in a rock band."

"You probably read about her. Zoe Madison? She sang with Freight Train when she was a kid and now her daughter's part of the band."

"You're friends with her?"

"She's part of my Wednesday-night gang, too. So you *have* read about her?"

"Who hasn't?"

Zoe's story had been written up by every tabloid on the planet, so Susan wasn't really surprised that Brian knew about her. They talked about Zoe awhile longer, Susan telling him how Zoe had traveled with the band, then gotten married to Zach Trainer's older brother. "It's like a fairy tale, isn't it?" she said when she was finished.

"I'm a cop. I don't believe in fairy tales."

Since they'd now reached Callie's and had parked his truck, Susan didn't answer until after they were inside the café and seated across from each other in a booth by the windows.

"Is it your job that's made you so cynical?" Susan asked.

He shrugged. "Susan, do you mind if we don't talk about my job?"

"Oh. Okay."

He sighed. "Look, I'm sorry, but some cops, they're a one-note tune. The job is all they can think about or talk about, and in my opinion have an inflated view of their own self-importance. Police work *is* important, but it's not my life."

Susan nodded. "I actually think that's a healthy attitude."

Now he smiled. "Thanks."

He turned to their waitress, who had approached, ready to take their orders. After ordering—a hamburger and side salad for Susan, a cheeseburger and fries for Brian—they resumed their conversation.

"So how's your week been?" he asked.

"Busy." She fiddled with her paper napkin, debating whether or not to tell Brian about his ex-wife coming into the shop. Finally she decided it would be the logical thing to do. "I met your ex-wife Thursday night."

He seemed startled. "Lonnie?"

"Yes."

"How'd that happen?"

"She came into the shop."

He frowned. "Why?"

"She said your daughter loved her brooch. I figured she just wanted to check out the shop." He was still frowning, and Susan knew he was thinking exactly what *she'd* thought—that Lonnie had wanted to check Susan out. "She's very nice, Brian."

"Yes, she is." His frown eased a bit.

"She bought a pair of earrings for herself and had me hold a matching bracelet. She said maybe her mother would buy it for her birthday."

He nodded, his eyes meeting hers. "You know, she probably heard about me taking you out."

"I kind of thought that might be the case."

"I'm sorry, Susan."

Just then their food came. Once the waiter was gone, Susan said, "Nothing to be sorry about." She began to cut up her salad greens into smaller pieces.

He studied her for a moment, and she wondered what he was thinking. For a while after that, they ate without talking. When the conversation resumed again, he seemed to have decided to keep it light and asked her interests. When she said she loved to read, he said he did, too, and for a while they talked about books and favorite authors. He said he preferred to read biographies and history, while Susan confessed to a liking for cozy mysteries.

"Nothing too gory," she said.

Over coffee and some of Callie's lemon meringue pie, a house specialty, they discovered they both loved to ride bicycles.

"Maybe we could go bike riding one night this week," Brian said.

"That would be fun." Susan felt a jolt of happiness that he was thinking in terms of seeing her again. "Mondays and Tuesdays are best for me."

"Let's say Tuesday night then."

"Okay."

By the time the waitress came with their bill, they'd decided he would drive over to her house on Tuesday about six-thirty, and from there they'd ride to the park, which was only two blocks from where she lived.

"Tell you what," she said. "I'll feed you after we're finished riding."

"Sounds good."

While he paid the bill, Susan went to the ladies' room, and by the time she came out, he was waiting for her near the entrance.

They didn't talk much on the way to her house— a ride that only took ten minutes.

"I've always liked this section of town," he said when he pulled into her driveway.

"Me, too." She wondered where he'd lived when he was married.

"When Lonnie and I were looking for a house, we wanted to buy here, near the park, but we couldn't find anything big enough."

"These houses *are* small. My friend Shawn—the one you met at Tony's—she and her husband live one street over, and she said it's really cramped now that they have the baby. There are only two bedrooms. And Shawn has a teenager."

"Yeah, that's the problem we ran into."

"So where *did* you buy?"

"Over in Oakcrest."

"That's a really nice area, too."

By now they had walked to her front door. Susan hadn't left an outside light on, but the moonlight and the glow from the streetlight on the corner provided enough light so she could see to unlock the door.

Turning back to Brian, she said, "Thanks for a great evening. I really enjoyed it."

"Mugger and all, huh?"

"Well, you have to admit it wasn't a run-of-the-mill date."

"No," he said, "there was nothing run-of-the-mill about it."

Something about his tone hollowed out her belly. She looked up. Time seemed to stand still. She was acutely aware of the cicadas singing in the trees, of the moonlight dappling the lawn, of the scent of recently mown grass and the faint perfume of the last of the summer roses in her neighbor's yard, but mostly she was aware of Brian.

Their eyes met and held.

He's going to kiss me....

The thought sizzled in the air between them. She swallowed, wanting him to kiss her more than she'd wanted anything in a long time.

But he didn't kiss her.

Instead he backed away, saying in a gruff voice, "Good night, Susan. I'll see you on Tuesday."

"I, um, good night."

What had happened? Disappointment flooded her as she watched him walk to his truck and get in. Why hadn't he kissed her? He'd wanted to. She knew he did.

She stood there until she could no longer see his taillights.

Only then did Susan open the door and go inside.

What the hell are you playing at? Brian asked himself as he drove home. Why can't you stick to a decision?

Once more he went over all the reasons that getting involved with Susan was a bad idea. *Remember, you have nothing to offer her.* His divorce had pretty much wiped him out financially, and he had no hope of changing that situation anytime soon. A cop simply didn't make much money, and no matter how many extra hours Brian picked up doing security for private parties or traffic control for churches or sporting events, there was seldom much left after he took care of his financial obligations.

He didn't begrudge a penny that he gave to Lonnie for the girls, nor did he begrudge her the house. In the divorce decree, once Janna graduated from high school—or if Lonnie should decide she wanted to sell sooner—the house would be sold, and he and Lonnie would split the proceeds. But Janna was only twelve. It would be six more years before Brian would see a penny of that money. And even then he would probably have to use the bulk of it to pay college expenses.

He sighed.

No matter how he sliced it, he was no prize for any woman. Hell, he doubted he'd ever be able to buy another house.

Unless you take Ed Grayling's offer...

Man, it was tempting.

But if he took that job, he'd have to travel around the state. And the hours would be 24/7, depending on the case. And what would that do to his time with the girls? And he couldn't discount lightly the fact he was only two years away from full retirement benefits with the town. Wouldn't it be crazy to forgo that when he was so close?

If you were smart, you'd call her on Monday and tell her something's come up and you won't be able to make it Tuesday night. Nip this thing in the bud.

And yet...

Susan.

He swallowed. *What if she's the one? What if she's the woman for me and I let the opportunity to find out go by?*

He couldn't stop thinking about how she'd looked tonight. About her smile. About the softness in her eyes when she looked at him. About the tenderness and vulnerability in her mouth.

About how much he'd wanted to kiss her.

And not just kiss her. Admit it, he thought. Admit how much you wanted her. The desire had been so great that when they'd stood outside her house in the moonlight, with the cicadas singing around them, and the fireflies lighting up the night, he'd had to fight against the strong temptation to just pick her up and carry her into the house and make love to her.

He told himself he was just horny. Going a long time without sex will do that to a man. And Susan was an attractive woman. A very attractive woman.

A sexy woman…

And she didn't even *know* she was sexy. As far as Brian was concerned, that lack of awareness made her even *more* appealing.

What am I going to do?

He wished he knew the answer.

Chapter Seven

"Brian, your father said you called and you won't be here for dinner Sunday." It was Monday morning; Brian had just arrived at the station.

"No, sorry, Mom. I'm working Sunday," he said into the phone.

"I thought you didn't work Sundays anymore."

"Max and Dotty had a chance to go to the races, and I said I'd cover for him."

"Somebody else could have done it," she said reproachfully.

Brian sighed. His mother seemed to think missing a Sunday dinner was on a par with committing a mortal sin. "I can use the extra money."

"Money. Money. That's all you ever talk about. If you hadn't divorced Lonnie—"

"Mom, I'm going to hang up now."

"Don't you *dare* hang up on me, Brian Patrick Murphy. Don't you dare."

Brian was afraid if he said what he was thinking, his relationship with his mother would be irreparably damaged. "I really do have to go."

"Fine," his mother finally said around a heavy sigh. "I guess if you can't come Sunday, you can't come." Then she brightened. "Maybe Lonnie can come with the girls."

Brian closed his eyes and counted to ten.

"That's perfect," his mother continued happily, "because I wanted to talk to her about the Outer Banks, anyway."

"Great, Mom." Then Brian snapped to what she'd just said. "The Outer Banks? What about the Outer Banks?"

"What do you mean, what about the Outer Banks? We're going for Thanksgiving, the way we always do."

"I know that. Why do you have to talk to Lonnie about it? The girls are coming."

"I know the girls are coming. I just think it would be nice if Lonnie could be there with us again."

Brian saw red. But he wasn't alone in the squad room. And he certainly didn't want his fellow cops or Jamie to hear him tell his mother exactly what he thought about this latest scheme of hers.

"Are you and Pop going to be home tonight?" he said through clenched teeth.

"Yes. Why?"

"Because I'm coming over after my shift is finished."

"What time will that be?"

"Seven o'clock."

"I'll save some roast for you." If his mother knew what he was thinking, she gave no indication of it.

"That's not necessary."

"I know it's not necessary. I want to."

"Fine. I'll see you later."

It was seven-thirty before Brian was finally able to get away from the station. Jeez, he'd never seen such a busy day. Or a more frustrating one. He'd spent the better part of the morning investigating a robbery that had taken place the night before but hadn't been discovered until the husband got home at eight. Apparently the wife was out of town and the husband had taken advantage of that fact and had spent the night elsewhere.

He kept begging Brian not to let his wife know he hadn't been at home during the night. "She'll kill me," he kept saying. "She'll kill me."

Brian didn't feel sorry for him. He had no sympathy for men who cheated. "She's bound to find out," he said. "It might be better if you just told her yourself."

And then, when he'd gotten back to the station,

he'd just had time to bolt down a sandwich before he had to hightail it over to the courthouse to testify in a juvie case in family court. That took longer than it should have, because the judge threw out the state's number-one piece of evidence. Then he'd barely made it back to the station in time to sit in on an interrogation that was linked to a case of his. And after that was finally over—with an unsatisfactory conclusion—he'd been snowed under with paperwork. And to top things off, at five o'clock, he'd had to attend a meeting called by the mayor, who was looking for suggestions about how to curb the increase in drug use by schoolchildren.

Brian liked the mayor, but he was tired, and he wasn't sure any program that didn't involve tons of money the city didn't have was going to solve the drug problem. The bottom line was, they needed more police officers. But without money, they weren't going to get them.

That job Ed had offered him was looking more and more attractive by the minute.

So he wasn't in the best frame of mind when he finally reached his parents' house at seven forty-five. He parked in the drive and opened the back gate. He could see his parents sitting at the kitchen table. They both had mugs in front of them. Their nightly hot chocolate, he was sure. It could be one hundred degrees in the shade, and they'd still have hot chocolate before they went to bed.

He knocked on the back door before opening it.

His dad carefully set down his mug. His hands didn't seem to be shaking tonight. "Hello, son." Maybe that new medication was working.

His mother smiled. "Oh, good, you're here." She immediately got up from the table and removed a cellophane-covered plate from the refrigerator. "I'll just pop this in the microwave for you."

Brian wasn't much in the mood for eating, and he wasn't sure his parents would want him to stay after he said his piece, but he also wasn't in the mood to argue with her, and he knew he'd get an argument if he tried to turn down food.

"Get yourself a beer, son," his father said.

"Sounds good." Brian walked to the fridge and grabbed a bottle of the ever-present Guinness.

"Hard day?" his father asked.

Brian sank onto a chair. "Yeah." At that moment he really wished he could talk to his father about Ed Grayling's offer, but the matter of Lonnie and the Outer Banks was more important right now. Maybe he could take his father to lunch tomorrow.

The microwave dinged, and his mother removed the plate of food and placed it in front of Brian. Then she bustled about, getting him a napkin, cutlery and the salt and pepper shakers. Finally she sat back down at the table.

Brian looked down at his plate. He had to admit the roast beef, mashed potatoes and green beans—which were probably fresh from his dad's garden—looked and smelled good. He cut a piece of meat and ate it.

His mother smiled happily. She loved feeding people, especially her family.

"Your father had a good day today," she said. "Didn't you, Mickey?"

Brian's father smiled. "I did."

"That's good, Pop. The new medicine's helping?"

"Seems to be."

They continued to talk about his father's progress and treatment for his Parkinson's until Brian finished his meal. "That was great, Mom. Thanks."

She beamed.

"But you know, much as I enjoyed the dinner, I didn't really come here to eat. I came to talk to you about what you said on the phone this morning."

"What do you mean?"

Brian was always amazed at how naive his mother could play it. She knew perfectly well what he meant. "About asking Lonnie to come to the Outer Banks over Thanksgiving."

"Sheila?" his dad said. "Did you ask Lonnie?"

Brian's mother lifted her chin and got that look on her face—the one that said *I didn't do a thing wrong.*

"*Did* you?" Brian's father said more insistently.

"Not yet, but why *shouldn't* we ask her? She's the mother of our granddaughters and as such she'll always be a member of our family."

Brian started to speak, but his father raised his hand to silence him.

"You know why we can't ask her," his father said. "She may be the mother of our granddaughters, but she's Brian's ex-wife. It's not fair to him to have her there."

"The girls want her," his mother said stubbornly.

"Have you talked to the girls about this?" Brian asked. He couldn't believe she'd do something so underhanded, especially when he'd thought they'd finally come to some agreement about Lonnie.

"No, but I know how they feel."

"Sheila—" his dad began.

Interrupting, Brian said, "Look, Ma. I'm only going to say this once. You can ask Lonnie to come to the Outer Banks for Thanksgiving, but if you do, count me out. And you can count the girls out, too, because Thanksgiving is my holiday according to Lonnie's and my custody agreement, so wherever I am, they'll be with me."

"You wouldn't disappoint them that way!" she cried.

"They won't be disappointed. Not if I take them to Disney World." Where he'd get the money to take them to Disney World over Thanksgiving, Brian didn't know, but he'd do it even if he had to raid his retirement account.

For a long moment his mother said nothing. Brian's eyes met his father's. Brian's father gave him a wry smile.

Finally his mother spoke, but not before sighing heavily. "You win, Brian. I won't ask Lonnie to come."

"Good. That's a good decision." Getting up, Brian carried his plate to the sink and rinsed it before placing it and his knife and fork into the dishwasher. He smiled at his dad, then turned back to his mother. "Thanks again for dinner."

Her eyes met his. Their gazes held for a long moment. Finally she pointed to her cheek.

Smiling, Brian walked over and kissed her. She was a tough one. For now, though, he'd won. But he wasn't kidding himself. This was only round two or three in their ongoing match. And until he figured out how to land a knockout punch, the fight would continue.

"So what do you think, Dad?" Brian and his father were having lunch at his dad's favorite pizza place, and Brian had just told him about Ed Grayling's offer.

"I don't know, Brian, me boy. It's a tough decision." Brian nodded.

"You've put in a lot of years with the police force," his father continued.

"Yes, I have."

"But you have to think about the welfare of your family."

"I know."

His father took a bite of his pizza and chewed reflectively. Outside the window of the shop, a mother walked by pushing a baby carriage. As she passed,

Brian could see the infant inside. The sight made him remember when Kaycee was an infant. He and Lonnie were so thrilled with her; they thought she was perfect, the most wonderful child that had ever been born. They'd have done anything for her. He sighed. His head told him the Grayling offer made sense. His heart wasn't sure.

"College is coming up for Kaycee in just a few years. How will you manage that?" his father asked.

"I don't know," Brian admitted. "I was hoping she'd get a scholarship, but her grades aren't quite good enough. She'll probably get a small scholarship through the patrolmen's union, but even going to a state school, we'll still be thousands short." Probably more like tens of thousands, he thought glumly. "I guess I could always borrow the money."

"I wish your mother and I could help you out, but you know our situation."

Yes, Brian did know. They had enough money coming in each month to cover their expenses, but they were afraid to spend their savings in case they needed it for when his father's Parkinson's got worse or some other medical emergency arose. Besides, Brian didn't want to take their money. His kids were *his* responsibility, not his parents'. They'd raised their children; it was his turn to raise his. "It's not your problem, Pop."

"This Ed Grayling. You like him? You trust him?"

"Yes."

"Then maybe you *should* do it, Brian. You'd still have your retirement with the police force. It might not be as much, but it sounds like you'd make up the difference quickly."

Brian nodded. What his father had said made sense.

"When do you have to let him know?"

"Sometime this week. He'll need to find someone else fast if I'm not going to do it, so I don't want to keep him hanging."

"Have you talked to Wayne about this?" Wayne Wilcox was the chief of police...and a lifelong friend of Brian's father.

Brian shook his head. "I don't want to until I've made my decision. Why? Does it make you uncomfortable?"

"No. This is too big a decision in your life. You have to make it without regard to my friendship with Wayne."

After that they finished their meal, and Brian drove his father home. Just before getting out of the truck, his father said, "I know you'll make the right decision, Brian. And whatever it is, you have my support."

As Brian drove away, he thought about how much he admired and respected his dad. He hoped that in all the years to come, his girls would feel the same way about him. Because in the end, being their father was the most important job of all.

* * *

Susan couldn't remember when she'd had such a good time. The bike ride with Brian was exhilarating—so much more fun than riding alone. They rode for an hour, part of it uphill, and by the time they were on their way back to her house, she could feel the workout in her calf muscles. She should ride her bike more often, she thought, resolving to do just that.

Now they were at her house, and she was getting dinner on the table. Yesterday she'd made a meat loaf, and while it was warming in the microwave, she cut up cucumbers and tomatoes and topped them with ranch dressing. Then she sliced a loaf of French bread, put out a wedge of soft cheese and took a container of potato salad out of the fridge.

"I'm starving," Brian announced as she set the warmed meat loaf on the table with the rest of the food.

"Well, dig in," Susan said.

Riding had given Susan an appetite, too, so for a while they were too busy eating to talk.

After two helpings of everything, Brian sat back with a satisfied groan. "Now I'm stuffed."

"So that means you don't want dessert, right?" She'd bought brownies at the bakery.

"Now I wouldn't go *that* far."

Susan grinned. "How about some coffee to go with the brownies I bought?"

"Personally, I like milk with brownies."

"Really? I'm a milk person, too."

Susan was glad she'd thought to buy another quart at the store.

"I'll help you clean up," he said when they'd polished off the last of the milk and brownies.

"You don't have to. There's not much."

"Don't argue, Susan. I'm helping."

She laughed, giving him a mock salute. "Yes, sir."

It only took fifteen minutes to put the remaining food away, clean off the table and wash and dry the dishes.

"There," he said, "aren't you glad it's done?"

"I am. Thank you for helping."

"Thank *you* for a great meal."

Susan made a face. "Meat loaf and store-bought potato salad isn't exactly gourmet fare."

"It tasted wonderful."

"You were just hungry." But she was pleased, for he'd certainly acted as if he liked the meal.

He glanced at his watch. "I guess I'd better be going."

The wall clock read ten-thirty. Susan couldn't believe it was that late already. The evening seemed to have flown by.

Because he'd parked in the drive, they walked out the back door to where his car was located. The scent of new-mown grass was strong in the air, and from somewhere nearby, a dog began to bark. Susan looked up. The harvest moon hung suspended in the inky sky like a huge silver dollar.

She breathed deeply. The air felt clean and new, so different from the heat of just a few weeks past. "I love autumn."

"Do you?" Brian's voice was soft.

They were standing at the edge of the drive; his truck was only a couple of feet away.

Something in his tone caused Susan's heart to skid. As their eyes met, Susan felt something radiate in the air between them. Something powerful. Almost as powerful as a charge of electricity.

For a few moments neither of them moved. And then, with a groan, he crushed her to him and lowered his mouth to hers.

Susan's head spun, and her knees felt weak as sensations pummeled her. When he deepened the kiss, she wound her arms around his neck and poured heart and soul into kissing him back.

How long they stood there, Susan didn't know. She only knew time and place and everything else in the world receded. There was only Brian. His touch. His taste. And how he made her feel.

"Susan," he murmured, finally breaking the kiss. "I'd better go."

"Yes. G-good night." She was so dazed, she couldn't think what else to say.

He kissed the tip of her nose. "Good night." His voice was husky. "I'll call you."

When he climbed into his truck, Susan slowly walked back into the house.

She stood in her kitchen, staring into space for a long time. There was only one thought in her head.

She could love Brian Murphy.

Maybe she already did.

Chapter Eight

Now you're in trouble, Brian told himself as he drove home. Don't you think you'd better decide how serious you are before you take this relationship with Susan any farther?

He smiled wryly.

Guess he should have thought about that *before* he kissed her.

That kiss.

It had awakened every single dormant hormone in his body. Brian couldn't remember wanting a woman as much as he'd wanted Susan tonight. In fact, it was a damn good thing he'd left when he had or he might have forgotten every single reason he had for not getting seriously involved with anyone, and carried her off to her bed right then and there.

Thank God something had stopped him.

But Brian knew if he continued to see Susan, he might not be so lucky a second time. For he was powerfully attracted to her.

So he had to come to a decision about her. And soon. And this time he'd better stick to it.

It took Susan a long time to fall asleep. She kept thinking about Brian. She knew he could be important to her. What she didn't know was whether it was wise to continue the relationship. If she thought they had a good chance of resolving the problems that existed between them, she wouldn't have a dilemma, because Brian was everything she'd ever wanted in a man.

But *could* they resolve their problems? The trouble was it was hard to know just how difficult these complications might turn out to be *without* going farther in their relationship. And the farther they went, the harder it would be to call a halt if the problems seemed insurmountable.

Damned if I do and damned if I don't.

She knew before she could make an intelligent, considered decision she needed to meet his girls and see if they would be receptive to her. But that wouldn't happen unless Brian wanted it to happen.

On and on her thoughts whirled. Finally, exhausted, she fell asleep.

When a shrill ring penetrated the fog of deep sleep, she thought it was the alarm, and she struggled to sit up. It was only then she realized the sound was the phone ringing.

Bleary-eyed, she looked at the digital clock on her dresser. It read 2:23. What in the world? Alarm raced through her.

Grabbing the phone, she clicked it on. "H-hello?"

"Susan?"

It was Sasha.

"Sasha! Where *are* you?" Susan cried, first relief, then alarm, flooding her. "Why are you calling me in the middle of the night? Is everything okay? I've been so worried. I've been calling and calling you."

"I know. I'm sorry." She sounded as if she were crying.

"If you know, why haven't you called me back?"

"I…I couldn't call you back." Now she was whispering. "He…he wouldn't let me."

"Who wouldn't let you?" But Susan knew. It was that boyfriend Brian had told her about. Oh, God, why did Sasha continually get taken in by losers?

"I…I'll tell you everything when I see you. Can I come there, Susan? I don't have anywhere else to go."

Susan didn't know whether to laugh or cry. To be furious or relieved. She sank onto the bed. She was so tired of Sasha's dramatics, of her problems, of her poor judgment, of her seeming inability to grow up. But how could she turn her away? Sasha was her sister, her only family. "Yes," she said wearily, "yes, of course you can come home."

Sasha's voice brightened. "It'll take me a while to get there cause I'm out of money and will have to hitch."

"Hitch! My God, Sasha, haven't you learned *anything*? You know it's too dangerous to hitchhike. Where are you, anyway?"

"Memphis."

"Memphis? What are you doing in Memphis?"

"It—it's where Gary...listen, Susan, I said I'll tell you everything when I see you, okay?"

Susan thought for a minute. Although the last thing she wanted to do was give Sasha any more money, what choice did she have? She certainly didn't want her sister hitchhiking. "I'll wire you some money," she finally said. "You can buy a bus ticket."

"Oh, Susan, thank you. You're the best. You won't be sorry. I promise you."

Susan had heard Sasha's promises before, and she knew how much they were worth. Still, she couldn't help hoping that maybe this time really would be different. Maybe Sasha really *had* learned a lesson. *And maybe the moon is made of green cheese.*

After making arrangements to wire the money the following morning to a Western Union office in west Memphis, they hung up, but not before Susan said, "Sasha, you *are* going to use this money to come here, aren't you?"

"Of course I am. Why would you say a thing like that?"

Susan ignored her sister's injured tone. "You know why. I've been burned before."

Back in bed, hoping she could fall asleep, Susan wondered what Brian would say about tonight's phone call. She knew what he'd think.

I hope he's wrong. But if he isn't, if Sasha lets me down again, it'll be the last time she does.

The next morning Brian stopped at Callie's for breakfast since he'd neglected to buy cereal or milk and didn't have anything else in the apartment that looked edible. He was glad no one he knew was at the café because he wasn't in the mood for small talk.

As he ate his pancakes and bacon, his thoughts returned to Susan, where they'd been ever since he'd left her the night before. He knew if he were smart, he would probably just cut off their relationship now. His life was too unsettled to take on a complicated relationship with a woman. But no matter how much sense that might make, Brian knew he couldn't do it. He had finally admitted to himself that he was falling in love with her.

This morning, when he'd first awakened, his first thought had been *She's the one*. And since then that thought had only become stronger.

They wouldn't have an easy time of it—both of them had too much baggage—but if they were going to build something permanent, they'd have to learn to accommodate it.

That meant he had to figure out the best way to introduce Susan to the girls and the rest of his family. He grimaced. It wouldn't be easy. He could just imagine his mother's reaction.

And the girls.

How would *they* react?

After finishing his breakfast, he motioned for the check. So what would be the best way to proceed? He couldn't spring everyone in his family on Susan at once. It would have to be gradual. And probably the best way to start was with his sister Caitlin. He and Caitlin had always been close. If she and Susan hit it off—which he was sure they would—then he'd have an ally and someone to help smooth the way with the rest of the family.

Yeah. That was a good plan.

Now that he'd decided what he wanted to do, he figured there was no sense in putting it off. Pulling out his cell, he punched in Caitlin's direct number.

"Caitlin Thomas."

"Hey, Cat."

"Hey, bro." Brian heard the smile in her voice. "What's up?"

"Have you got a few minutes?" In the background Brian could hear voices. Cat's agency was always jumping, no matter the time of day.

"For you, always."

"I need your help."

"Okay."

"I met this girl…woman…and I really like her. A lot."

"Well, well, well. That sounds serious."

"It could be. But there are problems."

Caitlin chuckled. "Namely our mother."

"Not just her. Maybe the girls, too."

"Yeah," Caitlin said softly. "They still hope you and Lonnie will patch things up."

"I know, but I think they'd be okay in time, as long as everyone else is. That's where you come in."

"What do you want me to do?"

That's what he liked most about his youngest sister. She was always in his corner, no matter what. She and Lonnie were close friends, yet she'd never allowed her feelings for her former sister-in-law to overshadow her love and respect for Brian. And she'd never acted as if she thought he had anything to be ashamed of or sorry for. She understood that the heart didn't always do the most sensible thing. Certainly it didn't do the easiest thing.

"I want you to meet Susan and help me ease her into the family circle."

"Okay. Tell you what. Why don't you bring her to meet Jack and me for dinner tomorrow night?"

"Can't be tomorrow. She owns that antique shop in the Mill Creek Center and she stays open late on Thursdays."

"We can't do it on Friday. How about Saturday?"

"That's good for me. And I'll check with her. If she can't make it then, I'll call you. Otherwise, where shall we go?"

"How about The Inn?"

The Maple Hills Inn was probably the nicest restaurant in the area. Brian hesitated. The prices at The Inn were a bit steep for his budget. But what the hell. That's why credit cards were invented, so people could live beyond their means. Until, he thought wryly, the piper came calling.

After deciding on seven-thirty—Caitlin saying she'd call for a reservation—they hung up.

Brian debated whether he should call Susan or just go by the shop. It wasn't a hard decision. He'd much rather see her in person than talk to her on the phone.

He grinned.

Who knew? Going to the shop, he might even be able to sneak in another kiss.

Brian just managed to make it to Susan's shop before closing time. He had tried to get there earlier; he knew she was meeting her friends for dinner at Callie's, and he didn't want to hold her up, but it had been another crazy, busy day at work.

"Brian! Hi." Susan's smile told him how happy she was to see him.

Brian's heart gave a little hop when their eyes

met. "Hi. I won't keep you long. I know you're going to dinner at Callie's tonight."

"Yes, but we don't meet until seven. I've got some time." Her face sobered. "I've been meaning to call you, anyway. I...I heard from Sasha last night."

"Oh?" He listened as Susan told him about the call, frowning when she admitted how late it had been when it had come through. That sister of hers was a real piece of work. He couldn't help comparing Sasha Pickering to his own sisters, all of whom were solid, upstanding citizens who worked hard and didn't expect handouts from anyone.

When Susan finished telling him what Sasha had said, he knew she wanted him to reassure her she'd done the right thing.

He sighed inwardly. "In your shoes, I'd have probably done the same thing," he finally said. "Time enough to get tough with her after she's back home."

Susan's relieved smile was his reward. Poor kid. He would've bet money she was in for another disappointment. "When will she get here?" he asked.

"I'm not sure. She's supposed to call me when she has her ticket and let me know when she'll arrive. A couple of days, I'd imagine."

He nodded. "When she does arrive, I'd like to talk to her."

"I figured you would."

He knew Susan was scared; he could see the fear in her eyes. Jeez, he hoped Sasha Pickering wasn't involved in the fraudulent charges on Susan's credit card. The last thing he wanted to do was to have to arrest her sister. That would make their other problems look minuscule.

"I talked to my sister this morning, too," he said. "And she's invited us to meet her and her husband for dinner on Saturday night. Would you like to go?"

He could tell from the way her eyes shone that she understood the subtext of what he was saying.

"I'd love to," she said.

"She's going to make reservations at The Inn."

"That sounds wonderful. The Inn is one of my favorite places."

He smiled. He wished they weren't in such a public place, because right now what he wanted most in the world was to walk around the counter, pull her into his arms and kiss her senseless.

"What?" she said, looking at him quizzically.

"Nothing," he said. "It's nothing." Then he smiled. "I'll see you Saturday night."

Deciding she couldn't go wrong with basic black, on Saturday night Susan put on a short black sheath and the pearls she'd inherited from her mother. She couldn't decide between black high-heeled sandals and her black suede pumps, but finally selected the pumps, then finished off her outfit with a black silk handbag to which she'd pinned an antique brooch studded with black and white rhinestones.

She wished she could do something different with her hair, but she wasn't the type for a chignon or upsweep or a funky short cut, so she contented herself with brushing her hair back from her face and securing it with a black velvet headband.

Looking at herself in the mirror, she decided she would have to do. She wasn't chic and trendy like Ann or sexy and beautiful like Shawn or worldly and sophisticated like Zoe. She was just herself, Susan Pickering, proprietor of a small antique shop in a small town.

But Brian knew that.

And he seemed to like her, anyway.

She had just spritzed herself lightly with her favorite fragrance when the doorbell rang.

Right on time, she thought, liking that about him. She had always believed that people who were chronically late believed their time was more important than anyone else's. Some of them even believed *they* were more important than anyone else. Susan was glad Brian wasn't one of them.

His eyes widened when she opened the door. "Wow," he said, whistling softly. "You sure look nice."

"I could say the same thing about you. In fact, I will say it. You look very handsome." An understatement, she thought. He looked gorgeous and sexy. In fact, he took her breath away in his dark-blue suit, pale-blue shirt and burgundy silk tie. Susan didn't know what it was about seeing a good-looking man in a suit, but it certainly revved her engines.

He grinned. "In other words, I clean up good."

"That, too."

"Better take a sweater or something," he said, eyeing the short, cap sleeves of her dress. "It's supposed to go down into the forties tonight."

"Yes, I heard the weather report." She reached for the little black fleece jacket she'd laid on the hall chair earlier.

As they made the twenty-minute drive to The Inn, Brian played the same "Asleep at the Wheel" CD he'd played the night they went to the movies, and once again, when "San Antonio Rose" began, the two of them sang along.

Susan smiled to herself. Was this going to be their song?

When they pulled into the circular driveway of The Inn, Susan could see the parking lot beyond was already three-quarters full. "Boy, they're busy tonight."

"This place is always busy," Brian said. "Not that I come here that often. But Caitlin does."

He handed his keys to the valet parking attendant, then came around to Susan's side to help her out of the truck.

Susan was trying not to be nervous over meeting Caitlin. Shawn had said she was nice. Still. Susan knew tonight was a test of sorts. Brian was testing the waters, seeing if Susan would fit in with his family.

All day long she'd told herself she had nothing to fear. She was smart, well educated and had held a very responsible position for many years before moving to Maple Hills. She could hold her own with anyone.

But no matter how many times she told herself all would be well, she couldn't banish the butterflies.

Walking into the elegantly furnished restaurant, the butterflies only became stronger.

A smiling blond hostess greeted them.

"Thomas," Brian said. "Party of four."

"Oh, yes. Mr. and Mrs. Thomas are already here. Follow me?" the hostess said, giving them another big smile as she led the way inside.

Susan loved The Inn. It was such a beautiful place, nestled among dozens of trees. Inside, it had dark-wood paneling on the walls, huge windows overlooking the landscaped grounds and plush furniture. The main dining room was designed around an enormous stone fireplace, and tonight a fire blazed brightly.

In one corner of the large room, an attractive older man played softly on a grand piano. The soft clink of silverware and muted voices of the diners provided a counterpoint to the music.

"Here we are," the hostess said, stopping at a window table on the right side of the dining room.

The couple seated at the table looked up. Susan decided she would have known the woman was Brian's sister without being introduced to her, for she was just a smaller, feminine version of Brian, with the same almost-black hair and vivid blue eyes. But where Brian was handsome, Caitlin Thomas was beautiful. Both she and her husband stood to shake hands with Susan as Brian introduced them.

Susan immediately liked both Caitlin and her husband, Jack, who seemed almost shy behind wire-rimmed glasses.

"I'm so happy to meet you, Susan," Caitlin said.

"Thank you. I'm happy to meet you, too." The name Jack Thomas seemed familiar to Susan, but she couldn't place how or where she'd heard it before. She knew she'd never met Caitlin's husband, for if she had, she was sure she would have remembered him, because he was very tall and thin. In fact, he looked like a runner.

Once they were all seated, a young waiter approached. "What can I get you to drink?" he asked, looking at Brian and Susan.

Susan noticed that Caitlin and Jack both had glasses of wine in front of them.

"I'd love a glass of Merlot," she said.

"I'll have the same," Brian said.

After the waiter left, there were a few moments of awkward silence, then both Brian and Caitlin spoke at once. They immediately stopped, laughing.

"Ladies first," Brian said.

"Well," Caitlin said, turning her gaze to Susan, "I was just going to say that Brian told me you own that antique shop at Mill Creek Center."

"Yes, I do," Susan said.

"I know exactly nothing about antiques," Caitlin said, "but I'm envious of people who do." She picked up her wineglass and drank some, her blue eyes studying Susan over the rim.

Susan wished she knew what Caitlin was thinking. She desperately wanted Brian's family to like her, but she'd learned a long time ago that you couldn't make people like you. They either did or they didn't, and it didn't pay to pretend to be someone you weren't. Just be yourself, Susan, had been her mother's advice ever since Susan could remember.

"Caitlin's in advertising," Brian said.

"I don't know a thing about advertising," Susan said with a smile, "so we're even."

Caitlin laughed. "Touché." Then she looked at Brian. "I like her."

"I like her, too," Brian said, reaching over and putting his hand on Susan's knee.

Susan knew she was blushing.

"Now we're embarrassing her," Caitlin said.

"Are we?" Brian asked.

"Yes," Susan said. "So let's talk about something else."

"When the Murphys gang up on you, you haven't got a prayer," Jack Thomas said.

"We never gang up on people," Caitlin said with mock indignation.

Jack rolled his eyes. "Wait'll you meet Sheila."

"Sheila?" Susan said, looking at Brian. He'd moved his hand away from her knee, but she could still feel its warm imprint.

"My mother," he said.

"Oh."

Just then their waiter came with Brian's and Susan's wine, and that gave Susan a few minutes to digest what Caitlin and Jack had said and what they hadn't said. She remembered now how Brian had mentioned his mother's feelings for Lonnie. Great. Susan had three strikes against her before she even began. She said a silent prayer that Caitlin really did like her, that she wasn't simply pretending because she wanted to put Susan off guard, get her to let down her defenses and maybe do or say something stupid. *God, you're paranoid.* But there was so much at stake, Susan couldn't help being nervous.

"How long have you owned your shop?" Caitlin asked.

Shaking off her negative thought, Susan told her an abbreviated version of her life.

"Hard to lose your mom so young," Caitlin said when she'd finished. There was real sympathy in her eyes.

Susan nodded. She still got a lump in her throat when she talked about her mother's untimely death. "Yes. It was."

"So how did you two meet?" Caitlin asked, looking at her brother.

"Well," he began, then gave Susan a questioning glance.

"I had a problem with someone charging stuff on

my credit card," Susan said, letting him off the hook. "I went to the police station to report the fraud the way the credit card company told me to, and Brian was the officer who talked to me."

"And you knew a good thing when you saw it," Jack said to Brian.

"I'm not slow," Brian said.

During dinner the conversation turned to Jack, who Susan discovered was an orthopedic surgeon affiliated with the county hospital. "That's where I've heard your name," she said. "I thought it sounded familiar. In fact, you were the surgeon who operated on a friend of mine. Gerri Mullins?"

"You know Gerri?" Jack asked.

"She works for me."

"No kidding. I've known her and her husband for years. They're neighbors of my parents."

"It's a small world, isn't it?" Susan said.

"Especially so in a small town," Caitlin said.

"Yeah," Brian said. "In fact, between us we probably know half the people in this dining room."

Caitlin and Brian, aided by Jack, kept the conversation moving throughout dinner, mostly telling funny stories about their large family. Susan was grateful the focus had moved away from her, because it made her uncomfortable to talk about herself for very long. Besides, she liked finding out more about Brian. She wondered if he realized how lucky he was to have such a close-knit family.

After dessert and coffee, the two women headed for the ladies' room, while the men took care of the bill, and while standing side by side in front of the mirror and repairing their lipstick, Caitlin's eyes met hers in the mirror.

Susan's heart skipped. What was Brian's sister thinking?

"There's something I need to know," Caitlin said.

Susan swallowed. "Okay."

"Do you love my brother?"

Susan could feel herself flushing. She hated that about herself. Why did her face have to show every single thing she was feeling? Because she wasn't the kind of person who could sidestep and evade, she simply told the truth. "Yes."

Caitlin nodded. "Good. That's good. Because I think he loves you. I have to warn you, though. It's not going to be easy. Are you up for the battle?"

"I…yes."

"You sure?"

"Yes," Susan said more firmly, "I'm sure."

"Okay. Then you can count on me to help."

After that there was nothing more to say, so Susan just smiled at Caitlin, who smiled back.

Later, in the truck heading for Susan's, Brian said, "So did you have a good time tonight?"

"I had a wonderful time. Caitlin and Jack are really nice people."

"Thank you. I think so, too."

For the rest of the drive, they listened to music and didn't talk. When they reached Susan's house, Brian pulled into the driveway and drove all the way to the back.

After helping her out of the truck, he put his arm around her waist and walked her to the back door.

This time when he turned her in his arms and his head dipped to kiss her, she was ready for the dizzying sensations that streaked through her like a lightning bolt. They stood there by the back door, pressed close together, and kissed over and over again.

When he finally lifted his head, they were both breathing hard.

"I want to make love to you," he murmured.

"That's what I want, too," she whispered back.

Lifting her chin, he looked deeply into her eyes. "Are you sure?"

"I've never been more sure of anything."

"Then what are we waiting for?"

Two minutes later, arms around each other, they climbed the stairs to her bedroom.

Chapter Nine

Susan didn't think she was very good at sex. She had listened to her girlfriends talk, and somehow she suspected they all knew something she didn't.

So even though she wanted Brian to make love to her, she felt awkward and was afraid she'd disappoint him.

"What's wrong?" he finally asked, when—after reaching her bedroom—she stiffened in his arms.

"I—" Susan swallowed. "It's been a long time. I...I'm scared."

"Of *me*?" he asked incredulously.

"No. I'm...I'm afraid I'll disappoint you."

"Susan, don't be silly. You could never disappoint

me. Besides…" He chuckled, kissing the tip of her nose. "I'm the one who should be scared. Guys are always worried we'll embarrass ourselves. I mean, it's hard being a guy. We're the ones who have to *do* something, and sometimes, well, the equipment doesn't want to work."

Susan couldn't help laughing. She laid her head against Brian's chest. She could feel his heart beating. She closed her eyes. She could trust this man. There was nothing to be afraid of.

"Susan?" he whispered.

She looked up.

"We don't have to be perfect." He smiled. "If we don't get it right the first time, we'll just try again until we do."

This time, when he kissed her, she quit thinking and just gave herself up to the thrilling sensations and emotions his kisses and then his touches elicited. Pretty soon, she had lost her shyness and was touching him back, marveling at how strong and solid he was—the kind of man you knew you could depend on, no matter what.

"Let's get these clothes off," he murmured, reaching for the zipper of her dress. Minutes later, naked, they lay tangled together in her bed.

Susan loved everything about Brian. She loved the curly hair on his chest. She loved the smell of him, the taste of him—so different, so male. She loved his big, capable hands that were so gentle when they stroked her. She especially loved the feel of him against her. She smiled at his erection, even as it excited her. She didn't think he had to worry about performing.

"Susan," he murmured, nuzzling her neck and then moving to her breasts where he captured first one nipple, then the other, gently tugging at them with his teeth. "You're so beautiful."

"No, I'm not," she said around a moan. It was hard to think, let alone talk, when he was doing such glorious things to her.

"Do you like that?" he asked, moving down to kiss and stroke her belly.

"Y-yes." She felt weak with desire.

When his hand moved lower, slowly inching between her legs, then probing until his fingers found the place that cried for his touch, she sucked in a breath.

"Relax," he whispered.

But she couldn't relax. Her body felt as if it was going to explode if he kept on.

"Please," she moaned, "I'm ready." She knew if he didn't stop, she was going to fall apart. She reached for him.

"Just let yourself go," he said, increasing the pressure and rhythm of his fingers.

And then, even though she tried to hold back, tried to wait for him, she couldn't, and she cried out as her body convulsed with wave after wave of intense pleasure.

Only then did he slip on a condom, then raise himself up and, parting her legs, slowly enter her.

"Oh," she said as he filled her up. It felt wonderful having him inside her. Even more wonderful when he began to move, pushing deeper with each thrust.

Winding her legs around him, she moved with him. Before long she felt that delicious buildup again. And this time when she climaxed it was only seconds before she felt him gasp and shudder, then collapse on top of her.

Afterward they held each other for a long time. Susan felt stunned and elated and happier than she'd ever felt before. If she knew anything, she knew she and Brian belonged together.

Later there would be time enough to worry about the problems they still faced. For now all she could think of were the words that kept running through her mind.

I love him. And I'm so thankful I've finally found him.

Brian drove home in a daze. He hadn't wanted to leave Susan, but he knew it wouldn't be a good idea to drive home after the sun came up. Too much of a chance that someone would see him. That was the last thing he needed, for the busybodies in Maple Hills to start gossiping about where he might have spent the night. He could just imagine what his mother would have to say. More important, he would never want his girls to hear about Susan or even a *hint* of Susan from anyone but him.

So at four o'clock, after the second, even better, time they'd made love, he reluctantly kissed Susan good night and headed out to his truck.

There was only one thought in his mind.

Now that he'd found Susan, he'd have to find a way to make her a permanent part of his life.

On Monday morning, first thing, Brian knocked on the chief's door.

"C'mon in."

Brian opened the door. Chief Wilcox looked up from some paperwork and smiled.

"Can I talk to you for a minute, Chief?"

"Sure. C'mon in. Sit down. What's on your mind?"

Brian closed the door before taking the chair in front of Chief Wilcox's desk. He took a deep breath. This was not something he looked forward to doing. "Before I type up an official letter, I wanted to tell you about something I've decided."

The chief frowned. "This sounds serious."

Brian nodded. "It is. For me, anyway. I've decided to leave the force."

The chief stared at him. "Tell me you're kidding."

Brian shook his head. "No, I'm afraid not. I've given this a lot of thought the past week or so, and although I wish it didn't have to be this way, I don't think I have a choice."

"Brian, I'm shocked. You...you're the best officer I've got. Hell, Brian, I thought you'd be the next chief of police when I retire."

Brian couldn't help feeling pleased at the compliment. "Thanks, Chief. I appreciate that, but I don't have any interest in the job. Never have."

Chief Wilcox looked at him steadily. "Why are you leaving, Brian? And is there anything I can do—we can do—to keep you?"

"No. I'm afraid not. I'm leaving because I can't take care of my family on the money I make as a cop. It was hard enough before, with two salaries, but now that I'm divorced, it's almost impossible. I'm broke all the time, and in the next few years, I'm going to have college expenses on top of everything else. And if I stay on the force, I might as well forget about ever getting married again."

"So what are your plans? What will you do?"

"I'm taking a position with Ed Grayling's firm."

The chief sighed. "I should have known. Damn."

"I'm sorry, Chief. This was a tough decision, but I think it's the right one."

"When are you going?"

"I'll tell Ed I have to give you at least three weeks. There are too many things hanging fire. Open cases. You know."

The chief nodded. "There's nothing I can do to change your mind, is there?"

Brian shook his head. "No."

"Well, I wish you a lot of luck, Brian. I hate losing you. But I understand."

Brian felt as if a huge load had been lifted from his shoulders, now that his decision had been made and he'd told Chief Wilcox about it. Even if things didn't work out with Susan, this new job was still a step in the right direction. Back at his desk he picked up the phone to call Ed Grayling and give him the news.

Susan was like a sleepwalker all day Monday. She kept replaying Saturday night in her head. Several times she picked up the phone to call Ann, then changed her mind. This thing with Brian was too new and too special. She didn't want to talk about it. She just wanted to savor it.

Brian.

He was so wonderful.

Perfect, in fact.

Well, not exactly perfect. After all, a divorced man with two daughters, one in her teens, and one almost in her teens, wasn't exactly her dream man, but considering everything, he was a pretty great guy.

Certainly, he was great in bed.

Susan smiled every time she remembered all the things they'd done Saturday night. She was amazed at herself, but she couldn't wait to do them again. Maybe they'd even try some *new* things the next time they were together.

And to think she hadn't thought she was any good at sex. Just proved that it only took the right man to bring out her hidden talents.

She was blissfully replaying the second time they'd made love—an even slower, more satisfying experience than the first one had been—when the bell on the outside door jangled, and she looked up to see Ann entering.

Susan felt as if she'd been caught with her hand in the cookie jar, and she blushed furiously. "H-hi," she stammered. *Idiot! She doesn't know what you were thinking about. Settle down.*

Ann gave her a curious look. "What's wrong with *you*?"

"Nothing. Nothing's wrong. I...I was just startled to see you."

Ann's eyes narrowed. "Susan, you've never been a good liar."

Susan sighed. "Oh, okay. When you walked in I was thinking about Brian. Specifically, about Saturday night. Anyway, you really *did* startle me."

Ann smiled. "So what happened? That's really why I stopped by. I have an appointment at eleven and had some time to kill, so thought I'd come get the nitty-gritty on the big date."

"And I'm dying to hear about *your* weekend." Ann had gone to visit her college roommate in Manhattan.

"You first," Ann said.

So in spite of her earlier thoughts about hoarding

the details, Susan ended by telling her everything. When she finished, Ann was grinning.

"I *knew* this guy was going to be important in your life," she said. "He sounds absolutely perfect for you." Then, grin fading, she added, "Do you love him, Susan?"

Susan nodded. "I think so."

"Then I hope everything works out for you."

"Me, too."

"I'm dying to meet him."

"I'm dying for you to meet him, too, but I don't see how that's going to happen anytime soon."

But the words were no sooner out of her mouth than the door opened and Brian walked in.

For a moment neither he nor Susan said anything. He looked at Ann, then back at Susan. She knew he thought Ann was a customer.

Finally Susan recovered from her initial surprise and said, "Brian, hi! Come on in. This is a friend of mine—Ann O'Brien. She's one of our Wednesday-night gang." Turning to Ann, she said, "Ann, this is Lieutenant Brian Murphy."

"It's nice to meet you, Ann," Brian said, smiling.

"The pleasure is all mine, Lieutenant." She stuck out her hand, and he shook it.

Brian's warm gaze met Susan's again, and the most delicious sensation slid into her stomach. She knew she was probably grinning like a fool, but she couldn't help herself.

"Well," Ann said brightly, "I need to be going. Don't want to be late for my appointment. 'Bye, sweetie," she said to Susan. "Goodbye, Lieutenant."

"'Bye, Ann."

As Ann walked behind Brian, she winked at Susan, then put her thumb and forefinger together in an O of approval.

When the door closed behind her, Brian said, "I should have called first, I guess."

"No, no problem. Ann really *does* have an appointment."

His eyes locked with hers. She loved his eyes. They were as blue as the ocean and just as deep.

"Susan..." he murmured huskily.

"What?" she whispered.

"I wish I could kiss you."

Susan's heart leapt. For a moment she was so flustered, she couldn't think what to say. She swallowed. "I...I have a back room."

Oh, God, his smile did things to her. Things that were probably illegal.

Trying to set a decorous pace, Susan walked toward the back, and he followed. Once out of sight of anyone who might come into the shop, he pulled her into his arms and settled his mouth on hers.

Susan closed her eyes as their tongues tangled. And when his right hand slid lower to cup her bottom and press her close, she almost wished she'd put the Closed sign out and locked the door.

"Susan, I haven't been able to think straight since I left you Saturday night," he groaned, his mouth moving to her neck.

"Me, neither."

"Can I come over tonight?"

"Yes."

"What time?" He kissed her ear, then ran his tongue around. "God, I want you." His erection pressed against her.

Susan wasn't sure she could wait until tonight. "Seven?" she said breathlessly.

"How about six-thirty?"

"Okay."

He kissed her again, then abruptly released her. "If I don't stop now, I won't be able to." Squeezing her hand, he said, "I'll see you later."

Susan nodded wordlessly.

A moment later he was gone, but she knew she would not be able to think of anything else but Brian and tonight for the rest of the day.

"Lonnie's going to be out of town this weekend, so the girls will be staying with me or I'll stay there with them. We haven't decided yet."

Susan turned her head to look at Brian. It was Thursday night. They'd spent every night but Wednesday together, and most of the time they'd been together, they'd been in her bed. She smiled. "I guess that means I won't be seeing you."

He kissed her lightly. "Not like this, but I'd really like for you to meet them. We'll be at my mother's on Sunday, but what about Saturday? Oh, you have to work on Saturday, don't you?"

"Actually, this Saturday I'm off. Gerri and I alternate Saturdays."

"Great! How about meeting us for lunch?"

"I—" Susan smiled. "Okay."

"I haven't talked to them about it yet, so I'm not sure how they'll react. I wanted to make sure it was okay with you first."

Susan knew he was warning her without making too big a deal out of it that things might not go entirely smoothly. It made her nervous just thinking about meeting his girls, especially since she knew they still hoped he and his ex would get back together. Still, if she hoped to be a part of Brian's life, she would have to bite the bullet sooner or later.

Maybe I'm worrying for nothing. Maybe they'll be perfectly fine knowing there's a new woman in their dad's life....

"The girls like China Garden. Is that okay with you?"

"Sure, that's fine, Brian."

"Okay, I'll tell the girls tomorrow night. But let's plan to meet at the restaurant at one, okay?"

"Okay."

"And, Susan?" He kissed her gently. "Quit worrying. Everything will be fine."

But Susan knew he was just saying that to make her feel better. Or maybe he was saying it because the alternative was not something he wanted to contemplate.

On his way home from work Friday night, Brian stopped by the house to talk to the girls. He found Janna in the kitchen mixing up a batch of brownies. Kaycee, as usual, was in her room talking on the phone.

"Mmm," he said, sticking his finger in the batter and licking it.

"Dad! There's raw egg in the batter. You shouldn't do that," Janna said, giving him a mock scowl.

Brian grinned. "Sorry. Did your mother get off okay?"

"Yeah. She left about thirty minutes ago, after giving us about ten billion instructions."

"Only ten billion, huh? She's falling down on the job."

"Hey, Dad, are you gonna stay here tonight?"

He knew the kids preferred to be in their own house, so even though it felt kind of weird sometimes, he didn't mind sleeping in the guest room. "Sure. I'll have to go home and get some stuff, but I'll stay here."

He sat at the table and watched her until she put the brownies in the oven. Then he said, "Honey, would you call your sister down? I want to talk to the two of you about something."

"Dad, she won't come if I call her."

"Tell her I want her. She'll come."

Janna sighed. "Okay," she said reluctantly. Still frowning, she left the room and he could hear her racing upstairs. Then he heard her banging on Kaycee's door.

"Kay*cee*!" she shouted. "Dad's here and he wants you to come downstairs."

A few minutes later Janna reappeared in the kitchen.

"Is Kaycee coming?"

Janna shrugged. "I don't know. She never answered me."

Brian got up and walked out to the hall. Standing at the foot of the stairs, he called up, "Kaycee, don't make me come up there."

A few seconds later Kaycee's door opened. "I'm coming," she said, irritation dripping from her voice. "I was on the phone. I couldn't just hang up on her."

Frowning, she clomped down the stairs.

Not a good beginning, Brian thought, following her into the kitchen.

"What're you making?" she asked Jenna when they entered the kitchen.

"Brownies," Janna said, "but you're on a diet so you don't get any."

Kaycee stuck her tongue out and muttered something that sounded suspiciously like, "Stupid."

"I'm not stupid. You are," Janna said.

"Stupid, stupid, stupid," Kaycee taunted.

"Girls," Brian said. "Please don't fight. I want to talk to you about something."

Kaycee gave him a wary look. "What?"

"Sit down, would you, honey?" *And quit frowning*, he wanted to add, *or your face might freeze that way*. It was something his mother used to say all the time when he and his sisters were growing up.

With a long-suffering sigh, Kaycee sank onto a chair. She looked at him.

Janna looked at him, too.

Well, it's now or never. Brian made his voice as casual as he could. "I, um, I've met someone I like a lot, and I'd like you guys to meet her, too."

Janna's expression was curious. "Like a girlfriend, you mean?"

Brian smiled. "Exactly like a girlfriend." But his smile faded when he turned to see Kaycee's reaction, for she looked stricken. He sighed inwardly. He had known this wouldn't be easy. "Kace, c'mon, don't look like that."

"How *should* I look? All happy? Well, I'm *not* happy, and nothing you say is going to *make* me happy." Her chin quivered.

Jeez, kids could make you feel lower than a worm sometimes. "Honey, I'm sorry. I know this isn't what you want, but can't you at least *try* to understand?"

"Oh, I understand all right." Her eyes glittered with tears. "You don't care how *we* feel or how Mom feels. All you care about is how *you* feel."

"That's not true and it's not fair. I care very much about how you feel."

"Then don't ask me to meet your new girlfriend."

"Kaycee…"

"I mean it, Daddy."

Brian's shoulders slumped. How could he have any kind of future with Susan if his children couldn't even talk about the possibility of someone else in his life? He thought about how just last night he'd reassured Susan that all would be okay. But what if it wasn't? What would he do then?

"I'll meet her, Dad," Janna said.

"Thank you, honey."

He and Janna both looked at Kaycee, who wouldn't meet their eyes. "Kaycee. Look at me."

Reluctantly she met his gaze.

"Just meet her, okay? That's all I'm asking."

Kaycee just stared at him.

"Please?"

Finally she shrugged. "When?"

"I thought we could meet her for lunch at China Garden tomorrow."

Her face was a picture of misery. "So soon?"

"There's no reason to wait, is there?"

She swallowed. "Who is she? What's her name?"

"Her name is Susan Pickering. She's the owner of the antique shop where I bought your brooch."

"Is that how you met her? Because you wanted to get me a birthday present?"

"No, I met her when she came into the station to report fraudulent use of her credit card."

"What time are we going tomorrow, Dad?" Janna asked.

Bless her, he thought. "I told her we'd meet her there at one." He smiled at Kaycee. "Then, if you want, I'll take you guys to a movie or something tomorrow afternoon."

"I have to study tomorrow afternoon," Kaycee said.

Brian knew this was her way of punishing him, for on his Saturdays, the girls never let anything interfere with their hours together.

Reaching across the table, he squeezed Kaycee's hand. "Well, I'm sorry you won't be able to go to the movies with me and Janna, but thank you for saying you'll meet Susan tomorrow."

She swallowed, avoiding his eyes.

Brian wished there was something else he could say to reassure Kaycee. But this was something she'd have to work out on her own.

For now he'd done everything he could.

Susan had thought she was nervous the night she'd met Brian's sister, but nothing compared to this. She arrived at the Chinese restaurant early because she did not want to walk in after Brian and the girls were already seated. She asked for a table for four by the window, and the pretty, smiling hostess led her to one of the two that were unoccupied.

Susan sat at an angle where she could see the main entrance from the window. That way she'd get a glimpse of Brian's girls before they came inside. She ordered a glass of iced tea and told herself to settle down. *They are just kids. How hard can this be?* But remembering Sasha at fifteen, Susan knew the meeting could be horrible. *Please God*, she prayed, *let things go well today*.

The waiter came with her tea, and she had just squeezed lemon into it when she saw Brian and his daughters approaching the entrance. She got a fleeting glimpse of a tall, slender girl with honey-blond hair and a smaller girl with dark hair.

Susan took several deep breaths. *Here we go*. A few seconds later, Brian and the girls entered the dining room. Brian spotted her immediately, and his face lit up. He spoke to the hostess, who led the three of them to Susan's table. Susan stood, her eyes meeting Brian's. "Hi."

"Hi, Susan." Drawing his younger daughter forward, he said, "This is Janna. Janna, this is Susan."

"Hello, Janna. It's so nice to meet you."

"Thank you. It's nice to meet you, too." She stuck out her hand, which amused Susan, who gravely shook it.

Susan couldn't get over how much Janna Murphy looked like her father and her Aunt Caitlin. The same dark hair, the same bright-blue eyes, even the same smile. Those Murphy genes sure were strong.

Kaycee Murphy, though, was a clone of her mother, Susan saw as Brian introduced them next.

Hair, features, build—they were very much how Susan remembered Lonnie. The only difference were her eyes, which were the same blue as her father's.

She politely shook hands with Susan, saying it was nice to meet her, but her smile didn't reach her eyes.

Susan's heart ached for the girl. It must be so hard to realize your mother and father weren't ever going to get back together when that's what you wanted most of all. And now she was being forced to meet her father's girlfriend.

Give me a chance, Kaycee. I'm not so bad. And I won't try to take your mother's place. I know I could never do that. Susan tried to telegraph her thoughts in the warmth of her smile. But Kaycee had already looked away, as if by not looking at Susan she could distance herself from the entire scene.

After they were all seated—Brian across from Susan, the girls between them—their waiter came to take their drink orders. The girls ordered sodas, Brian iced tea. His gaze met Susan's across the table, and she smiled to show him she was fine. She knew he was worried. A lot was at stake here. She was worried, too, but she was wise enough to know this was only a beginning. They would have a long road ahead of them.

After the waiter left them, Brian said, "Have you been waiting long?"

"No, only a few minutes."

Turning to Janna, Susan said, "Your dad tells me you're in the seventh grade this year."

"Uh-huh. And boy, it's much *harder* than sixth grade was."

"Janna's taking an eighth grade course, too," Brian explained.

"Really?" Susan said. "Which one?"

"Spanish I," Janna said with a proud smile. "It's my favorite subject, too."

"That's great. Spanish is the perfect language to learn. And what about you, Kaycee? You're a freshman, right?"

"Yes."

"What's *your* favorite subject this year?"

She shrugged. "Music, I guess."

"Kaycee's in the chorus this year," Brian said. Turning to his daughter, he added, "Susan sings in her church choir."

"I'm a second soprano," Susan said. "What do you sing?"

"Alto." Her cryptic answers didn't invite further discussion. Not looking at either her father or Susan, she picked up her menu, opened it and began to study it.

This wasn't going to be easy, but then, anything worth having usually wasn't. Susan's eyes met Brian's briefly, then she, too, picked up her menu.

Once they'd decided what they wanted, Brian signaled their waiter. "We're sharing, right?" he said as the waiter walked toward them.

"I don't like to share," Kaycee said. It was the most words she'd strung together since arriving.

"Kayce…" he said gently.

Her throat worked.

Oh, God, Susan thought. This was a big mistake. Kaycee wasn't even close to being ready to acknowledge another woman in her father's life.

"I like trying some of everything," Janna said.

Susan turned to her gratefully, giving her a smile. Janna was a sweetheart.

Kaycee seemed to get herself under control again, and when the waiter came, she placed her order for cashew chicken calmly.

After the waiter left again, an awkward silence fell. Then Brian, in an obvious attempt to lighten the atmosphere, said, "I'm glad you decided you can go to the movies after all this afternoon, Kaycee. Have you picked what you want to see yet?"

"I want to see the new Harry Potter movie," Janna said. Then she made a face. "But Kaycee doesn't."

"What's your choice, Kaycee?" Brian said.

Kaycee shrugged. "I don't know," she mumbled.

And so it went until their food came. Brian kept trying to draw Kaycee into the conversation, but she wasn't going to be drawn.

At least now that they had their food, they had something else to do besides talk.

"The lo mein is great," Brian said.

"All the food is good," Susan said.

"I like the lemon chicken the best," Janna said.

Kaycee said nothing.

"I think I like the cashew chicken best," Susan said brightly. "I'm glad you ordered it, Kaycee."

In answer, Kaycee only nodded.

Susan's spirits sank. Today had been a gargantuan mistake. These girls—well, Kaycee, anyway—were no more ready to accept her in Brian's life than they were to accept coals in their Christmas stockings.

She couldn't wait until this lunch fiasco was over. She glanced at Brian. She could see from his expression that he felt the same way.

Oh, Brian, what are we going to do?

Somehow they made it through the rest of the meal. Then, just as Susan began to think that maybe the worst had happened and the only direction they could possibly go was up, Kaycee clutched her stomach. "Dad," she said, "I don't feel good."

"What's wrong? Are you sick to your stomach?"

She nodded, her eyes filled with misery. "Can you take me home?"

Susan could see Brian didn't know what to do. "It's okay, Brian. Go ahead."

"But—"

"Please, Dad," Kaycee said, her eyes filling with tears.

Brian gave Susan a helpless look.

Go, she mouthed.

I'm sorry, he mouthed back.

She nodded, giving him a sympathetic smile, although she was sick at heart.

"Go on out to the car," he said to Kaycee. "I'll pay the check and be there in a couple of minutes. Janna, you go with her."

"Okay, Dad."

"I hope you feel better soon, Kaycee," Susan said.

"Thanks." She didn't meet Susan's eyes.

"'Bye, Susan," Janna said.

"'Bye, honey."

After the girls walked out, Brian leaned down and gave Susan a brief kiss. "I'll call you later."

"All right."

Susan went into the ladies' room while Brian paid the bill, and when she came out he was gone. She was glad. She needed time to think.

She'd been so hopeful about meeting his girls.

But after today she wasn't sure any amount of time would make a difference in the way Kaycee felt about her.

She was terribly afraid her relationship with Brian was doomed.

Chapter Ten

Mom, I miss you so much.

Susan had been sitting by her mother's grave for a long time. After leaving the restaurant, she'd stopped to buy some flowers, then she'd headed straight for the cemetery. Now the flowers sat in a small vase that fitted into a holder at the base of her mother's gravestone. The yellow and orange mums looked bright and cheerful, just like her mother had been when she was alive.

For the past half hour, Susan had been telling her mother about Brian and his girls and what had happened today and how she felt about all of it. Then she'd told her about Sasha and the credit card and how much she hoped Sasha wasn't involved.

One part of Susan's mind knew her mother couldn't hear her, but the other part, the part that still believed in miracles, thought maybe her mother *could* hear her, and maybe she'd send Susan some of her wisdom.

God knows Susan could use it.

"I wish I knew what to say to Sasha," she said. "I know if you were here, you'd have the perfect words. I keep thinking about what a sweet little girl she was and how much she loved you. I have to believe that sweet girl is still somewhere inside of her, and if I could just think of the right things to say, I'd find her."

"You okay, ma'am?"

Susan started. A thin old man dressed in overalls and a flannel shirt, obviously a caretaker of some sort, stood on the walkway a few feet away. He had a rake in his hands and a concerned expression on his face.

"I'm fine," she said.

"I heard you talkin' and I just wondered, that's all."

Susan smiled sadly. She gestured to her mother's grave. "My mother's buried here. Sometimes I just come here to talk to her."

He nodded. "Okay, well, I'll leave you be, then."

As he walked away, Susan thought about getting up and going home. Instead she gazed out, across the cemetery to the lake beyond. On the other side of the lake, which rippled in the afternoon breeze, lay the city park. It was such a peaceful scene, a perfect place to sit and think.

Her mind drifted, and she remembered how happy

her family used to be. She thought about how, in the evenings, her mother used to sit and read to Sasha, who loved the poems of Shel Silverstein. Susan loved them, too, but she thought she was too old for them, so she pretended to be engrossed in a book of her own, even though she was listening just as intently as her little sister.

Sasha always wanted to hear the same two poems, the one about the boy who turned into a TV set and the one about the girl who turned into a whale. She'd giggle no matter how many times their mother read them to her, and Susan would hide her own smile behind her book.

In the winter there would be a fire in the fireplace, and sometimes, before their mother settled down to read aloud, she'd make hot chocolate and put miniature marshmallows in it. Sometimes they'd have popcorn or graham crackers to go along with it.

Until Susan became an adult, she hadn't realized just how rare and wonderful her mother was. Although Hazel Pickering could have been bitter about becoming a widow at such a young age, she had never allowed that sad loss to affect her positive approach to life.

Even when she got sick and knew she was dying, she remained upbeat and encouraging. One of the last things she'd said to Susan was how glad she was to know she was leaving Sasha in such good hands and that she knew the two of them would always be close and there for each other.

I'm so sorry, Mom. I know I've let you down.

Hearing voices, Susan saw a couple approaching. Sighing, she rose and dusted herself off.

It was time to go.

"I hope I didn't wake you."

It was almost eleven o'clock. Susan *was* in bed, but she'd been reading—if you could call it that. She'd been having a hard time concentrating on her book—even though it was a new thriller by Harlan Coben, one she'd looked forward to reading—because her thoughts kept zigzagging between the afternoon's disastrous luncheon and her worries about Sasha. She sighed. "No, Brian," she said, "I wasn't asleep."

"Good. I wanted to call earlier, but one of the girls always seemed to be around. So I waited till they went to bed. I'm really sorry about what happened today, Susan."

"Me, too. How *is* Kaycee? Feeling better?"

"She started feeling better as soon as she got home. I guess I was expecting too much today. It's obvious it's going to take time for her to adjust to having another woman in my life."

If she ever does...

"I'll work on her, though." When Susan didn't say anything, he said more urgently, "Promise me you won't give up on us."

"No, I...I won't."

"You don't sound sure."

"I just…I don't know…today depressed me. The thing is, I understand how Kaycee feels. And I don't blame her for feeling that way, either. She's just a kid, Brian, and her world's been turned upside down in the past three years. Another change, especially one of this magnitude, is frightening to her. I'm sure she's scared of losing you completely."

"I know. I realize I need to reassure her. But I think she'll come around once she gets used to the idea and understands it's not going to change our relationship."

"I hope you're right." The trouble was, if Susan and Brian were together, it *would* change his relationship with his girls. It had to. Yes, he'd still love them and spend lots of time with them, but Susan would be there, too. Not all the time, of course, but a lot of the time. Because she couldn't *have* a relationship with him unless she was included in his family life. But she hesitated to say all this, at least not now. After all, he'd never even said he loved her. She knew he did; he let her know in so many ways. But still…the words hadn't been said. They'd only been implied.

"I wish I was there with you right now," he said softly.

Without warning, Susan's eyes filled. "I wish you were here, too," she whispered.

"I'll still have the girls all day tomorrow, so it'll be Monday night before I can come over. Is that okay?"

"Yes, that's fine."

"I'll pick up some steaks, maybe we can grill them."

"Sounds good."

After they hung up, Susan swiped at her tears. She was angry with herself. What was wrong with her, anyway? It wasn't like her to be weepy. It also wasn't like her to be negative. Who knew? Maybe Brian was right. Maybe all Kaycee needed was more time.

In the meantime, maybe Susan had better work on her *own* family problems. She still hadn't heard from Sasha, even though she'd tried calling her when she got home this afternoon. The really disturbing thing was that instead of getting Sasha's voice mail, Susan had gotten a recording saying the number she'd called was no longer in service.

Although Susan didn't want to admit it, Sasha had probably used the money she'd sent her for something other than a bus ticket to Maple Hills.

Now what? she thought.

If only she knew what to do.

Unfortunately, there was no one she could turn to for help. She had no doubt about what her girlfriends would say. They'd tell her to forget about Sasha. Write her off. They'd say she'd had enough chances, taken advantage of Susan long enough.

And Brian...

Susan swallowed. Brian would probably say something even stronger.

I'm all alone in this.

Susan walked into the living room. Picking up the

framed photo of her mother from where it sat on top of the spinet piano, she lovingly studied her mother's sweet smile and wise eyes.

And suddenly Susan knew exactly what her mother would say if she were there. The same thing she'd said so many times after Susan's father died.

It's just us now, girls. All for one and one for all, just like the Three Musketeers.

Susan put the photo down. She really didn't have a choice. She could never abandon Sasha. No matter what she might have done. No matter how long it was before she contacted Susan again.

Sasha was her sister.

And as long as Susan was able, she would be there for her.

After leaving his parents' home where they'd had dinner and played a raucous game of charades with the rest of the Murphy clan, Brian dropped the girls at the house. He'd been back at his apartment for about an hour and was brushing his teeth in preparation for bed when the phone rang. He hurriedly spit out the toothpaste, wiped his mouth on a towel and headed for the phone.

"Brian? It's Lonnie."

"Oh. Hi, Lonnie."

"Sorry to call so late."

"That's okay."

"Um, I was wondering if maybe we could meet for

lunch tomorrow. There's something I wanted to talk to you about."

Uh-oh, he thought. Kaycee and Janna had told Lonnie about yesterday's lunch. Sighing inwardly, he said, "Sure. What time?"

"Can I give you a call in the morning? After I see Doc Redding's appointment schedule?"

"Sure, that's fine."

"Okay, talk to you in the morning, then."

After they hung up, Brian finished getting ready for bed. He couldn't help speculating over what Lonnie would have to say the next day. Jeez, why did everything have to be so damned complicated?

Was Lonnie going to get on his case for upsetting Kaycee? He hoped not. The last thing he wanted to do was discuss Susan and his feelings for her with Lonnie.

Damn.

He was not looking forward to this lunch.

Lonnie called a few minutes after Brian arrived at the station on Monday.

"It looks like I can meet you about 12:30. Will that work?"

"That's perfect. Where do you want to go?"

"How about Peterson's Cafeteria?"

"Okay. See you there."

The morning flew by. Brian knew the remainder of his days with the force would all fly by, because he had too much to do and not enough time to get it all done. His coworkers still didn't know he was leaving. Brian planned to tell them this afternoon when he gave Chief Wilcox his official letter of resignation.

In fact, no one except the chief and Ed Grayling knew about the change in jobs. He would probably tell Susan when he saw her tonight. And once he'd told his parents, then he'd tell Lonnie and the girls.

At noon he started cleaning up his desk. He left the station at 12:15, telling Jamie where he'd be. When he pulled into the parking lot at the cafeteria, he saw Lonnie just getting out of her little Subaru. She waved at him.

He parked his truck and walked over to meet her. She looked very professional in a navy pantsuit and white blouse, her blond hair tied back with a navy-blue bow. They walked into the cafeteria together, and Brian couldn't help thinking how many times they'd been there before.

The line wasn't very long, so they made short work of selecting their food. Brian found them a booth, and they unloaded their trays. A busboy took them, and Brian and Lonnie sat across from one another.

Brian waited until Lonnie had sweetened her iced tea and buttered her roll, then plunged in. "So what's up, Lonnie? Did Kaycee tell you about yesterday's lunch?"

"Yes, she did, and so did Janna."

Lonnie didn't seem upset. That was a good sign. "What did Kaycee say?"

Lonnie ate some of her salmon croquette before answering. "She's not very happy, as I'm sure you realize. But I talked to her about it, tried to reassure her."

"You did?"

Lonnie smiled. "I know this will surprise you, Brian, but I'm actually very pleased that you've met someone."

He was surprised, but he tried not to show it.

"Because," she continued, "I've met someone, too."

Brian's mouth fell open. He couldn't have been more stunned if she'd told him she was joining a nunnery.

"And I've been afraid for him to meet the girls, so we only see each other when they're spending the night with you or when they both have plans." She grinned. "Why are you so shocked?"

"I don't know. I shouldn't be. Thing is, I would have thought my sisters would have said something."

"They don't know."

"They *don't?*"

"No." At this she looked sheepish. "Truth is, I've been kind of reluctant to tell your family."

He nodded. "Yeah, I can understand that. The only one who knows about Susan—by the way, that's her name—is Caitlin. I was hoping she could help me ease the way with the rest of them." He made a face. "Especially my mother."

"Susan. She's the owner of the antique shop, right?"

"Yeah." He cut a piece of fish.

Lonnie smiled. "I liked her, Brian. She seems like a really nice woman."

"She is." He ate some of his potatoes. "So who's the guy you're seeing?"

"His name is Ethan Ross. He's a pharmaceutical salesman."

"So you met him at work?"

She nodded.

"Does he live in Maple Hills?"

Lonnie shook her head. "No. He lives in Banning. He's divorced, too. But he doesn't have any children, which makes it a bit easier."

"I'm glad for you, Lonnie. I just hope this guy's good enough for you."

"He's a really good guy, Brian. I think you'd like him. And I want you to meet him. After all, if we get married, he'll be the girls' stepfather."

"Are you talking about getting married?"

"Yes, we are."

For some reason it gave Brian an odd feeling to think of her married to someone else, even as he was happy about it. He guessed that, considering how long he'd been married to Lonnie, it was simply hard to envision her as part of another couple. He realized, though, that this was pretty hypocritical, considering that he was hoping for her support on the issue of bringing Susan into his life.

"Anyway," she said, "I just wanted you to know what's going on. Now that you've broken the ice with the girls, I'll introduce Ethan to them soon. I think that'll make it easier for you and Susan."

Brian knew this was only the first step toward making things work, but it was a big one. He went back to the station feeling more positive about his relationship with Susan. In fact, he couldn't wait to tell her what Lonnie had had to say.

Now if only Susan's sister would contact her. He knew she was worried about Sasha. It had been six days since Susan had sent her the money for her bus ticket, and no word. Damn. He was hoping against hope that he was wrong about Sasha, but things didn't look good.

They didn't look good at all.

Late that afternoon, just before Brian quit for the day, he got a phone call from Allmark Visa, Susan's credit card company. The man he talked to said they had been able to secure a photo of the person who had made one of the fraudulent purchases on her card. "It's not high quality. It came from a security camera tape. But you can still see about three-quarters of the woman's face."

"Can you fax me a copy?" Brian asked.

"That's the reason I called. I'd like you to show the photo to Miss Pickering. See if she might recognize the woman."

"There's something that doesn't add up here," Brian said. "Miss Pickering still has the card in her possession. How'd this woman make the purchase without the card itself?"

"Apparently," the Allmark representative said, "we sent it to her."

"You *sent* it to her?"

"Yes." His voice was rueful.

"How'd *that* happen?"

"Well, several weeks after notifying us of a change of address, a woman we believed to be Miss Pickering called us and said her card had accidentally been damaged and she needed a new one. We mailed her one."

"At the post office box address."

"Yes."

Jeez, Brian thought. The criminal mind never ceased to amaze him with its ingenuity. He'd often thought if that ingenuity had been turned to productive work there was no telling what good things might have been accomplished. "That explains it, then." He was more sure than ever that Susan's sister was behind this clever scheme, but hoped he was wrong.

Before hanging up, Brian gave the man the fax number at the station. He didn't have to wait long. Within ten minutes, the photo came through. It was grainy, but you could see the woman's features and enough of her body to know she was slender.

Brian studied the woman's face carefully. It was obvious she was young, more a girl than a woman. He thought about the framed photo Susan kept on her dresser. He couldn't be positive, but the girl in this picture looked an awful lot like Susan's sister.

He shook his head. He knew Susan was going to be crushed. He wished he wasn't involved. Of course, he thought wryly, if he hadn't become involved, he wouldn't ever have met Susan.

He folded the fax carefully and put it in the inside vest pocket of his jacket. Then, sighing, dreading being the bearer of bad news, he said good-night to Jamie and headed for home.

After showering and changing into jeans and a knit shirt, Brian drove to Susan's. On the way he stopped at the supermarket and bought two rib eye steaks and, while he was at it, mushrooms, hard rolls and a bottle of wine. What the hell, might as well make the bad news more palatable. Besides, he hoped they'd celebrate both what Lonnie had told him and his new job.

As always, he pulled into the driveway and parked close to the garage. When he walked to the back door, he could see Susan in the kitchen. He smiled, watching her for a few moments before knocking.

She turned at his knock, came over and unlocked the door. Her smile said how glad she was to see him.

Bending down, he gave her a lingering kiss— drawing her close with his right arm while still holding the bag of groceries in his left. She smelled like flowers and her lemony shampoo and something else—something that was uniquely Susan.

"Hey," he said softly, letting her go.

"Hey, yourself."

"I brought offerings." He held out the groceries.

"Thanks." She took the groceries and carried them over to the counter.

Brian removed his jacket and hung it over the back of one of the kitchen chairs. Walking up behind her, he slid his arms around her waist and nuzzled her neck.

She sighed.

"I couldn't wait to get here tonight," he murmured, pulling her hair back and nipping at her ear.

"Brian…" Her breath hitched as his hands slid up to cup her breasts.

Turning her around, he pressed against her and kissed her deeply. He knew she could feel how much he wanted her. "Let's go upstairs," he muttered.

"Aren't you hungry?" she managed to say before he kissed her again.

"Right now all I'm hungry for is you," he said when he let her up for air.

Five minutes later they were undressing each other, tossing their clothes wherever they landed, heedless of everything except the urgency of their need.

Later, cradling her in his arms, Brian said, "I've got two pieces of good news. At least I hope you'll think it's good."

"You won the lottery."

He laughed. "Not quite."

She laughed, too. "Well, c'mon, don't keep me in suspense."

So he told her about Lonnie's call and their conversation at lunch today.

"That *is* good news, Brian. Although I'm not sure Kaycee will think so."

He grimaced. "I know. Poor kid. I can't help feeling sorry for her."

"Me, neither." She sighed. "So what else? You said two pieces of good news."

"I gave three weeks' notice today."

"Brian! I can't believe it. You mean, you're no longer going to be a cop?"

"Only for the next three weeks."

Then he told her about the offer Ed Grayling had made him and how he'd finally decided to take it. "So what do you think?" he asked when he'd finished.

"Well, I'm glad for you, of course, if this is what you want. But Brian, I thought you…" She stopped.

"What?"

"I thought being a cop was important to you."

"It has been. Believe me, this wasn't an easy decision. But, Susan, I have to be able to support my family." *And if we want to be married…* But it was too soon to say anything like that.

"I understand."

"Anyway, I'm kind of excited about this. It should be interesting and challenging. I think I'll enjoy it."

"Then I'm happy for you, Brian."

He grinned. "Then what do you say we go open that bottle of wine and celebrate?" Time enough, he thought, to show her the picture of the girl he was afraid was Sasha after they'd had some wine and a nice meal.

"That was so good," Susan said. She smiled across the table at Brian. "I love the way you made those mushrooms. They tasted wonderful."

"All I did was slice 'em up, cook 'em in a little butter, add some garlic bread sprinkle and soy sauce."

"I know. I watched you." She loved when he smiled at her like that. "Want me to make some coffee?"

He shook his head. His eyes met hers.

For some reason Susan felt a twinge of alarm.

"I have something to show you."

Susan waited. Something was wrong.

He reached for his jacket and removed a piece of paper from the inside pocket. Handing it to her, he said, "This was faxed to me this afternoon by your credit card company. It's a photo of a young woman, taken by a security camera, as she made a purchase using your credit card."

Susan's heart knocked against her chest as she opened the paper and looked at the picture. She swallowed. The picture wasn't all that clear and only showed part of her face, but Susan would know her anywhere. The woman in the picture was Sasha. There was no doubt about it. Telling herself to keep her expression neutral, Susan raised her eyes.

"Do you recognize her?"

Susan's heart hammered at the thought of the little girl she'd helped to raise being sent to jail with the roughest types of criminals. She felt sick to her stomach from the ugly images that ran through her brain. She hesitated for a long moment before shaking her head and saying, "No."

Brian gave her a searching look. "You're sure?"

Her mouth was so dry, it was almost impossible to answer, but she forced herself to say, "I'm positive."

She knew he didn't believe her. She could see it in his eyes. She hated lying to him, but what else could she do? She'd already decided she could never betray Sasha, no matter what Sasha had done, even though knowing without a doubt that her sister was the one who had made all those charges against her credit card just about broke Susan's heart.

Keep it together until he leaves. Don't let him see how upset you are.

Susan got up from the table and began clearing their dishes. "I shouldn't have had three glasses of wine," she said. "Now I have a headache."

"Maybe I should go," he said.

She nodded, not meeting his eyes. "Maybe you should. I think I'll take a couple of Advil and go to bed. Get a good night's sleep."

He stood then, too, and picked up his plate and cutlery. For a moment he just stood there, then he walked over and placed them on the counter by the sink where they joined hers. "Susan."

Slowly she met his gaze.

"Are you okay?"

The caring in his voice was nearly her undoing. "I'm fine. It's just this headache, that's all."

"Okay." Leaning over, he kissed her gently. "I'll call you tomorrow."

She nodded. All she had to do was hold it together for a few more minutes. Just a few more minutes.

After putting on his jacket and tucking the fax containing the photo into his pocket, he opened the back door, said he hoped she slept well, and then he walked out.

Susan locked the door and began to load the dishwasher. She carefully kept her mind blank.

But when she saw his headlights back out of the drive and knew he was finally gone, she began to shake.

Sinking down onto a chair, she buried her face in her arms and let the tears come.

Chapter Eleven

She'd lied to him.

Brian knew Susan had recognized the girl in the photo as Sasha. He'd seen the involuntary stiffening of her shoulders and the way she'd avoided his eyes. He was disappointed that she didn't trust him enough to tell him the truth, yet he reluctantly understood.

Sasha was all the family Susan had. She felt responsible for her and protective of her.

Now he had a serious dilemma. In a normal situation, if he suspected a particular person of a crime, he'd notify the appropriate party—in this case, the credit card company.

But this wasn't a normal situation. This was Susan,

the woman he loved. The woman he hoped to make a permanent part of his life. And the person in question would, he hoped, someday be his sister-in-law.

This is why you should never have gotten personally involved with Susan. Now if you do the job you're supposed to do by law, you will jeopardize your relationship with her. And if you don't do your job, you are betraying the oath you've taken to uphold and enforce the law.

When he woke up after a restless night, he was still trying to find a way out of the problem—a way that wouldn't hurt Susan but would still allow him to do the right thing—and he was no closer to a solution.

All morning he stewed over the problem. Finally he realized he had no real choice. He had to confront Susan. There was no other way.

If he hadn't already made plans to go to lunch with Rick Foley, a fellow cop, he'd go to see Susan at the shop. But maybe it was a good thing he couldn't see her on his lunch break. On reflection, it would be better to wait until tonight, for he was sure she'd get upset when he told her he believed she'd lied to him. Not a good thing to do to her when she'd still have hours of customer interaction ahead of her.

For the remainder of the day, he tried to put the problem out of his mind. Now that he'd made his decision, it wasn't difficult, because he was extremely busy. After the lunch with Rick—who wanted to know everything about the new job and made no bones of the fact he was envious—Brian had to go to court to testify in a hit-and-run case. That took most of the afternoon, so by the time he cleared up everything else on his desk, it was nearly six-thirty before he left the station.

He knew Susan sometimes didn't make it home before seven, especially if she had errands to run on the way, so he decided to stop by his parents' house and tell them about the new job before going over to see her.

"Brian!" his mother exclaimed. "I can't believe you're leaving the force." She turned to Brian's father. "Mickey? Aren't you surprised?"

Brian's eyes met his father's.

"Brian told me last week that he was considering taking this job," his father said.

His mother's mouth dropped open. "And you didn't tell *me*?

Brian smiled. "I'm telling you now, Ma."

She gave a huff of indignation. "I meant your father."

"Brian asked me not to say anything," he said.

"But surely you didn't mean not to tell *me*," she insisted.

"Ma, what difference does it make?" Brian said. He walked over to where she stood drying dishes and gave her a hug.

She gave him a stern look. Then she laughed. "I'm not mad. Actually, I'm very proud of you, putting your family first. What did Wayne have to say? I'll bet he was shocked."

"He wasn't real happy about it, but he was a good sport," Brian said. He went on to tell them what the chief had said about thinking Brian would be the next chief of police.

"And why not?" his mother said.

Brian smothered a smile. His mother thought all of her children were exceptional. Maybe all mothers did.

They talked awhile more, then Brian glanced at the clock. It was seven-thirty. "I should go," he said. "I've got some things to do."

"We'll see you on Sunday?" his mother said, walking him to the door.

"I'll be here." Brian thought about saying he might be bringing someone with him, then changed his mind. Better to wait and see how things went with Susan tonight. She might not be speaking to him on Sunday.

It was almost eight o'clock when Brian finally pulled into Susan's driveway. Out of habit, he circled around back and parked in front of the garage. There were lights on in the kitchen, so she was home. Walking to the back door, he knocked.

A few minutes later she turned the outside light on and peered out. Smiling quizzically, she opened the door. "Brian, I didn't expect you."

"I know," he said, giving her a quick kiss. "I wanted to talk to you about last night. I'm sorry, Susan, but I know you recognized the girl in that picture I showed you."

At his words, a telltale flush appeared on her face.

"The girl was Sasha, wasn't it?"

"It wasn't Sasha."

"Look, I understand how you feel, but you're not doing your sister any favors. She needs to be held accountable for what she's done or she'll never be a responsible person. If she gets away with this, who knows what she'll do the next time. Do you want to take that chance?"

She stared at him, and he saw the doubt and torment in her eyes. And then, just as she started to say something else, the doorbell chimed. "I...I have to get that."

"Go ahead." He knew she wanted him to leave, but he'd be damned if he was going to. They had to settle this. Tonight. "I'll wait right here."

But when she walked out of the room, some instinct he would later question made him follow her.

Susan knew Brian was behind her when she walked into the hallway and headed for the front door. The doorbell pealed again. She was grateful for the interruption. Maybe by the time she got rid of whoever it was at the door—probably some kid selling something—she would be composed enough to once more deny Brian's accusation.

She snapped on the front light, then opened the door. And stared.

Oh, God, no...

It was Sasha who stood there.

Shock kept Susan immobile for precious seconds. Then, fear clutching her heart, she tried to hide Sasha by standing in front of her so Brian wouldn't see her, but she immediately knew it was hopeless.

Of course he'd seen her.

How could he help but?

There was nothing Susan could do except let her sister in.

"Jeez, Susan, I didn't think you'd *ever* answer the damned door," Sasha said. Her eyes were bleary; she looked exhausted. A huge duffle bag was slung over her shoulder, and the moment she stepped into the hallway, she dropped it on the floor. "Man, that thing was heavy. I've been lugging it—" She stopped, and by the way her eyes narrowed, Susan knew she'd finally seen Brian standing there. "Oh, hey. Sorry. Didn't see you there," she said.

Susan slowly turned around. Her eyes met Brian's. For a long moment neither moved.

Susan swallowed. "Please, Brian?" They both knew what she was asking.

For agonizing moments, Brian looked torn. Susan could see the indecision on his face. *If you love me, don't do this.* If only she could say the words aloud. Yet would they do any good?

The grandfather clock chimed the quarter hour, and the sound seemed to galvanize Brian.

"I'm sorry, Susan," he said.

Then, walking forward, he took Sasha by the arm

and said, "Sasha Pickering, you're under arrest for fraud. You have the right to remain silent. Anything you say can and will be used against you in a court of law. You have the right to speak to an attorney, and to have an attorney present during any questioning. If you cannot afford a lawyer, one will be provided for you at government expense. Do you understand?"

Sasha, eyes huge with terror, looked at Susan. "Sissy?"

Susan's eyes filled. Sissy was Sasha's baby name for Susan. She hadn't used it in years. "I'm so sorry, honey."

Sasha burst into tears. "I trusted you!" she cried. "You betrayed me!"

"Oh, Sasha, I didn't, I—"

But Sasha cut her off. "I hate you! I hate you!" She tried to wrench her arm away from Brian, but she was no match for his strength and size. He'd already whipped out his cell phone and was speaking into it.

"I need a squad car at…" He went on to give Susan's address. When he clicked the phone off, he looked at Susan again.

Susan was so upset she didn't care what he thought. "Brian, please, don't do this. I…I'll pay the balance owed to Allmark. If the money's paid back, there's no crime, right? Call the station back, tell them it was a mistake, tell them you don't need a squad car or anything else."

"Susan, you know I can't do that."

"Why not?" she cried.

"First of all, it's too late. Allmark has already reported the loss and has an ongoing investigation underway. I'm sorry. I love you, but your sister broke the law. She committed a third-degree felony, and I know it. I'm a cop. I can't ignore what she's done."

The words *I love you*, words Susan had longed to hear, were empty now. Because if Brian *really* loved her, he would forget about being a cop. If he really loved her, he'd let Sasha go.

"If you do this," she said, fighting back tears, "don't bother to come back."

He stared at her. "You don't mean that."

"I do mean it."

All through this exchange Sasha continued to weep. Susan walked over and put her arms around her. When she did, Brian let go of her arm. Sasha's whole body was trembling, and for a moment she resisted Susan. Then with a cry she clung to Susan.

"Don't worry, Sasha," Susan said. "I'll call this attorney I know. Everything will be all right. I promise you."

"Don't let him take me away," Sasha cried.

But even as she was begging Susan, they all heard the sound of a siren coming closer.

"You know," Caitlin said. "In Susan's shoes, I'd've told you to get lost, too."

Brian winced at her blunt words. It was now

Thursday, two days since he'd arrested Sasha Pickering. One day since Susan had bailed her out of jail. A lifetime since she'd talked to him, or at least it seemed that way.

"I know you did your job, Brian, but in a situation like this, a woman wants to know that she's more important than your job."

"She *is* more important than my job, Cat. But hell, you know I couldn't ignore the law—or what she'd done to Susan. What kind of sister does what Sasha did? She didn't care about Susan, yet somehow it's now all my fault. How is that fair?"

"I know. I'm just saying…" She shrugged, giving him one of those sorry-you're-screwed expressions.

The two of them were having lunch together. It was one of those rare days when Caitlin had been working with a customer in Maple Hills and had called him to see if he was free.

Brian picked at his French fries. "So what do you think should I do?"

"I'm thinking flowers, chocolates, poetry, abject apologies, declarations of undying love accompanied by a huge diamond—and anything else you can think of."

"Flowers, chocolates, abject apologies and undying love I can do," Brian said glumly. "Huge diamonds are out of my price range. And poetry? You're kidding, right?"

She smiled, polished off the last of her chicken

Caesar salad, then took a twenty-dollar bill out of her purse and put it on the table. "I've got to run. Good luck and keep me posted, okay?"

He picked up the twenty and tried to give it back to her. "Lunch is on me."

"Don't be silly. I'm the one who called you, remember?"

"So?"

"So?"

"Fine," he finally said. "Next time I'll buy."

After he got back to the station, he kept thinking about what Caitlin had advised.

Maybe I should *send her flowers*. After all, he reasoned, she couldn't hang up on flowers.

Because he didn't have a better idea, Brian grabbed his jacket, told Jamie he'd be back in thirty minutes, then drove two blocks to Paula's Posies.

Paula Maxwell, the owner of the florist shop, looked up as he entered. She smiled. "Hi, Brian. Long time no see."

Brian and Paula had gone to high school together. "Yeah, it has been a while."

She brushed her dark hair back. "So what brings you here?"

"I want some flowers. Something really nice."

"What's the occasion?"

"Nothing special. I just want to send someone flowers."

Paula smiled. "A woman?"

Oh, hell, he might as well tell her. She was going to know, anyway, since he planned to have the shop deliver the flowers. "Yeah, a woman."

"Okay, how about roses? Those are always appropriate."

"I'd like a mixture of flowers. You know, a bouquet. Something really pretty."

"Do you have a top dollar limit? That'll make a difference."

"Sixty or seventy dollars?"

She thought for a minute. "I can put together something really nice for that. I'm thinking a mix of pink roses, pink stargazer lilies, purple freesia, white asters, and yellow oncidium orchids. Something like that will be delicate and beautiful."

He nodded, relieved. "That sounds good." He had no idea what freesia or stargazer lilies or even asters looked like, but it didn't matter. He trusted Paula.

"How'd you want to pay for this, Brian?"

He dug out his wallet. While she was ringing up the sale, she told him to look at the available cards and pick one. Brian chose one that had a thin silver border and was otherwise blank. On it, he wrote: "I am so sorry I hurt you. Please forgive me. I love you. Brian."

Then he put the card in its envelope, sealed it, wrote Susan's name on the outside, then handed the card to Paula.

"We can deliver these this afternoon, if you like."

"That would be great. They're going to Susan

Pickering at Hazel's Closet, the antique shop at the Mill Creek Center."

"Really? Susan Pickering? I had no idea you two were an item."

"Do you know Susan?"

"I do. She and I sing in the church choir together."

Brian should have known in a town the size of Maple Hills, he would constantly run into people who knew Susan, especially since she ran a local business.

"You have good taste, Brian," Paula said. "Susan's a really nice gal."

"Thanks. I think so, too."

As Brian drove back to the station, he decided he would call Susan again tonight. She'd refused to talk to him yesterday when he called her at work, but maybe after getting the flowers she would relent and at least talk to him. And if she wouldn't, he guessed he'd have to try something else. Because one thing he knew for sure. He wasn't going to give up without a fight.

Susan was waiting on a customer who seemed really interested in a set of Lenox dinnerware when the bell on the door jangled. She looked up to see a young man holding an enormous vase of flowers.

"Miss Pickering?" he said. He put the flowers down on top of the glass case that contained jewelry.

"Yes," she said, walking to the front.

"These are for you. Please sign here." He held out a clipboard and Susan signed her name.

After he left, Susan glanced back at her customer.

"You go ahead," the woman said, "I'm fine on my own."

Susan looked at the flowers. They were beautiful. She was fairly sure Brian had sent them, but they could have come from Ann or one of her other girl-friends. By now, they all knew what had happened. She reached for the card.

She fought for control as she read what he said. Conflicting emotions surged through her. Pain and anger were dominant.

What did he think? That he could spend a few dollars on some flowers and write a few words on a card and everything would be okay again? Things between them would *never* be okay again. Couldn't he see that?

Susan thought about Sasha at home. How frightened she was. How her eyes were red and swollen from crying. How she'd begged Susan to help her. They still hadn't talked about the whys of what Sasha had done; in fact, Sasha had denied having anything to do with the crime until Susan had told her she'd been photographed by a security camera. Then her face had crumpled, and she'd just kept saying, "I'm sorry, I'm sorry. Please don't let them send me to prison, please, Susan."

Susan sighed, thinking of what Stella Vogel, the attorney that Shawn worked for, had told them. Apparently, whether or not Sasha was sentenced to a jail term was pretty much going to be up to the judge. According to Ohio law, what she'd committed was a third-degree felony, because the amount she'd defrauded the credit card company out of fell between five and twenty-five thousand dollars.

"She *could* get up to five years," Stella had said.

Sasha's face went white.

"I don't think you will," the lawyer had continued. "This is a first offense and I think the judge will take the nature of the crime—the fact it was nonviolent—and your youth into consideration. Also, if Susan vouches for you, that should help, too. But…I won't lie to you. If we get a hard-line judge, and there are a few of them, you might have to serve some time."

Sasha's bottom lip had quivered, and Susan reached for her hand. She couldn't bear to think of Sasha in prison, no matter *what* she'd done.

"Um, Susan?"

Susan jumped. She'd forgotten all about her customer. "Oh, I'm sorry." Pushing thoughts of the consultation with Stella out of her mind, she walked back to where the woman, a fiftyish redhead, stood. "Is there something else you'd like to ask me?"

The woman smiled. "Nope. I've decided to take the set."

As Susan rang up the sale and found a box big enough to pack up the set, she decided she wouldn't acknowledge Brian's flowers. In fact, as soon as her customer left, she intended to throw them in the trash.

* * *

Brian found himself driving by Susan's shop anytime he was out during the day. And he did the same thing at night, only then he drove by her house. Jeez, he thought. He was acting like a lovesick teenager.

Two weeks had now gone by since the night he'd arrested Sasha. Two weeks during which he'd had one hell of a time concentrating on work or anything else, because all he could think about was the pain in Susan's eyes the last time he'd seen her.

Although she'd never know it, he'd talked to Joe McCormick in the county prosecutor's office and asked him to personally oversee Sasha's case. Brian knew Joe was a good guy who had teenage girls, one of whom had given him some trouble, so he figured Joe wouldn't take a hard line with Sasha.

Sometimes Brian wondered what might have happened if Sasha had only come home a few weeks later, when he was no longer a cop.

But there was no sense wondering about what-ifs. What was done was done, and now Sasha's fate—and Brian's, too—was in the control of the courts.

All Brian could hope for was that she got a good judge, one who wouldn't throw the book at her but would instead give her a short sentence in a minimum-security prison where she would get counseling.

* * *

Susan had lost weight in the past two weeks. It was no wonder. Her appetite had completely disappeared. And she wasn't sleeping well, either.

All she could think about were Sasha and what was going to happen to her and Brian and how much she missed him.

Sasha was now helping Susan in the shop, because she had to do something until her court date, and working for Susan seemed the best solution.

Sasha was doing surprisingly well. It was obvious to Susan that her sister was scared out of her mind and determined not to do anything that would make her circumstances worse than they were. And she was surprising in other ways, too, ways that gave Susan hope that things really would be different now.

One night, after a dinner of baked chicken and salad—which Sasha had made while urging Susan to relax—Sasha said, "Susan, I want you to know that even though Gary was no great shakes, it wasn't his idea for me to use your credit card." She put a finger in her mouth, then hurriedly took it out again. Biting her nails was a nervous habit that she was trying to break. "I'd like to blame it on him, but Stella said I needed to face up to what I've done if I hope to get leniency from the judge when my case comes up."

Susan nodded. Stella *had* said that, and much more. In fact, she'd been tough with Sasha and had emphasized how she needed to show real remorse when they went to court. She'd also told Sasha that how she spent this time waiting for her case to be heard would weigh heavily with the judge.

"If you work hard and show that you've learned your lesson and are trying to change, I think that'll go a long way toward getting you a lighter sentence," she'd said.

Susan could see that Sasha had really taken her stern words to heart. "So why *did* you run up all those charges?" she asked. "Just for a lark?"

Sasha's eyes, so like their mother's, clouded. She looked away, then sighed and looked at Susan again. "I was pissed at you."

"At *me*? What did *I* do?"

Sasha grimaced. "Nothing. But—"

"But what?" Susan asked, genuinely confused.

"You've always been so *perfect*," Sasha said. "And I was always such a loser. Even when I tried to do things the way you did—like get good grades and take part in school activities—I always screwed up."

"Sasha! How can you say that? You were *never* a loser."

"Yes, I was. I still am, but I'm trying to change."

"Oh, Sasha…" Susan got up from the table and walked around to where Sasha was sitting. She bent down and put her arms around her sister. "Honey, I hate to hear you talk about yourself like this. You're a wonderful girl. You're beautiful, you're talented, you can do anything you want to do if you'll just believe in yourself."

"I couldn't be a model."

Susan sighed. She pulled up a chair and sat next to Sasha. "Becoming a successful model isn't something you can just do because you want to. It's a highly competitive business, and the odds are staggeringly against you. You tried, and I give you credit for that. But just because it didn't work out doesn't mean you're a failure."

A tear rolled down Sasha's face. "I wish…"

"What, honey? What do you wish?"

"I wish I was kind, like you are."

"Oh, Sasha." Now Susan felt like crying, too.

Sasha knuckled her tears away. "I'm so sorry, Susan. For everything."

Susan smiled. "I know you are."

"Can you ever forgive me?"

Susan reached for Sasha's hand. "I already have."

That night, as Susan lay in bed, she thought about everything Sasha had said. And for the first time since the night her sister had been arrested, Susan wondered if maybe Brian had been right after all.

Chapter Twelve

Susan stared at the spreadsheet on her monitor and sighed. There was no way around it. She was going to have to borrow money against her house.

Even though she'd had a successful customer-appreciation sale, the five thousand dollars she'd had to pay the bail bondsman to keep Sasha out of jail until her court date had wiped out all of her profits, and the retainer she'd given Stella Vogel to represent Sasha had pretty much taken care of the rest.

Not only did she not have the money to expand or get an online store set up, she didn't have enough operating capital to last her until the holiday surge replenished the coffers.

And there were two fall shows she wanted to attend—one in Columbus two weeks from now and the other in Cincinnati early next month. There'd be no point in going if she didn't have the money to buy anything.

Susan swallowed. Her house had never been mortgaged. Her mom had paid cash for it using the settlement from her father's company after his fatal accident. And it had always been a source of comfort to Susan to know that, if all else failed, she and Sasha both had a mortgage-free roof over their heads.

But there was no help for it. She would have to call her bank. The only good thing about borrowing money against her house was the fact that home mortgage interest rates were lower than for any other kind of loan.

Standing and stretching—it had been slow this morning so she'd spent most of it at the computer paying bills and working on her budget—she looked out the front windows. It was hard to believe it was already the second week of October. Almost a month now since Sasha had come home. *Since I've seen or spoken to Brian.*

He no longer called her, but could she blame him? She wouldn't speak to him in the days following Sasha's arrest, and then she had ignored the flowers he'd sent, so he'd obviously gotten the message.

He's changed his mind about me. He's realized that I come with baggage, too, and he no longer wants to be associated with me. After all, what would his family, especially his daughters, think about a woman whose sister is a felon?

These were the thoughts that had tormented her for a while now. Because if Brian still felt the same way about her, if he really loved her despite everything, wouldn't he have kept trying to patch things up, no matter how many times she'd rebuffed him?

You only have yourself to blame if you've driven him away for good....

Several times in the past week, Susan had almost gotten up enough courage to call him, to at least *see* if they still had a chance, but each time she'd backed away at the last minute. Her emotions were too fragile right now. She wasn't sure she could deal with hearing that he no longer wanted her.

Because as long as the words weren't said, there was still a smidgen of hope.

"We're on the docket."

Susan's heart jumped at Stella's words. "When?"

"They've set Sasha's date for the fifth of next month at nine in the morning. And it's Judge Hawkins's court, thank God."

"Judge Hawkins is a good judge?"

"She's one of the best. She's not a pushover, but she's very fair, and she seems to have a soft spot for kids. Also, the nine-o'clock start time is lucky."

"Why is that?"

"Because if you're scheduled for later in the day, there's always a chance the court will run overtime and you'll be rescheduled for another day. With an early time, we'll be sure of getting in."

Susan guessed she was glad, although in some ways, just like the situation with Brian, it was better not to know what the future held. "Stella, what do you think is going to happen?"

"Honestly? I don't know. But I do think because this is a first offence and because Sasha is pleading guilty and is showing true remorse, not to mention working and keeping her nose clean, Judge Hawkins will go easy on her."

"I can't wait to tell Sasha."

"Where is she? I wanted to talk to her."

"I signed her up for a two-week computer course at that new technology school that opened up in June. I figured that would help her find a job when all this is over."

"Good thinking. What time are her classes over?"

"She'll be here by two o'clock."

"Have her call me then, okay? We'll need to set up an appointment to go over exactly what she can expect at court. It's best not to have any surprises. I want her fully prepared."

"Thank you, Stella. We're both so grateful to you for your help."

"It's my pleasure, Susan. Let's just hope the outcome is as favorable as we want it to be."

After they hung up, Susan wished she had someone to share this news with—someone who cared about Sasha as much as she did. But there wasn't anyone.

If only I could talk to Brian about this.

Tears filmed her eyes, which infuriated her. Why was she still crying over him? Their relationship was over. *Deal with it, Susan.*

"Dad? Are you busy?"

"Yes and no," Brian said into his cell phone. "What's up, Kaycee?"

"What do you mean, yes and no?"

He smiled. "I'm on a stakeout. It's boring as h— heck."

"You can say hell. I've heard the word before."

"Don't be a smarty-pants." But he was grinning.

"I thought only cops went on stakeouts."

"I should have said surveillance."

"Oh."

Brian heard a sigh. His tone sobered. "Is something wrong, Kaycee?"

Another sigh. "I don't know. Dad? Why does everything have to change all the time?"

"That's life, honey." An image of Susan as he'd seen her last filled his mind. "It's constantly changing, whether we want it to or not."

"I *hate* change."

"That means you hate getting older. You hate the thought of dating. Of going to college."

"I don't hate *those* things."

Out of the corner of his eye, Brian saw movement in the driveway of the home of the subject he was watching. "Honey, I've gotta go. I'll call you later, okay?" Brian had already started the truck.

"Okay," Kaycee said. "Tonight?"

"Yes, tonight." Disconnecting the call, Brian put his cell phone on the seat beside him and waited. A minute later, a black Honda Accord backed out of his subject's drive. Since the only person living in the house was the male he was being paid to watch and report on, Brian waited until the Honda was almost to the end of the block. Then he pulled out and followed.

He'd been on this particular assignment for more than a week. The company that had hired Ed's security service wanted to know if this man—one of their top employees—was selling industrial secrets to a rival company.

So far, Brian had discovered nothing that would indicate the employee was disloyal or dishonest, but even though he was bored silly with sitting, watching and following—with no discernable success—he figured as long as someone was willing to pay him the nice, hefty sum they were paying him, he could keep it up forever. Tomorrow, though, he'd make sure he brought his Walkman.

The only downside of an assignment like this—besides the boredom—was that he had too much time to think. Mainly about Susan. But also about his girls, who were growing up. And Lonnie, who was getting married. And Sasha Pickering. Whose court date was coming up soon. And all the mistakes he'd made in his life.

He sighed. He hoped he'd learned from those mistakes, just as he hoped Sasha Pickering would learn from hers.

As far as his kids were concerned, all he could do was try to help them deal with the problems and temptations they'd be faced with in the future—and if they stumbled, he needed to be there to pick them up.

What about Susan?

Unfortunately, Brian couldn't think of anything he could do right now that would make a difference to Susan. Everything in their future—if they even had one together—hinged on what would happen to Sasha.

Something that was now completely out of Brian's control.

It was after seven before Brian got home. After changing into jeans and a sweatshirt, he put on worn running shoes and, cell phone in hand, struck out for a walk. Maybe he could get rid of the kinks and stiffness caused by too many hours spent sitting in his truck.

He headed for the park.

On the way he punched in the speed dial for his old house. Naturally, Kaycee answered. If she was anywhere in the house, no one else ever had a chance when the phone rang.

"So what's on your mind, kiddo?" he asked.

"Mom and Ethan have set a date," she said glumly.

"Yeah, I know."

"You *do*?"

"Yeah, your mom told me."

"Dad, why can't you and Mom be like other divorced people? It's kind of weird that you act like you're friends."

Brian laughed. "I would have thought you'd *like* that we're friends, Kaycee."

She sighed. "I do. I just—I don't know. Why do things have to *change*?"

"I think we talked about this earlier."

For a few moments she didn't say anything. Then, "Where *are* you anyway?"

"I'm in the park. Walking."

"Oh. Dad?"

"Yeah, Kaycee?"

"If…if you want to let Susan come along Friday night when we go to Tony's, it'll be okay with me."

Love streamed through Brian. "Thank you, honey, that means a lot to me, but I don't think that's going to work out."

"Why not? Oh, she probably hates me, doesn't she?"

"No, Kaycee, she doesn't hate you." *It's me she hates.* "I, um, well, Susan and I aren't really seeing each other anymore."

"You're not? But I thought you really liked her."

"I do."

"Then what happened? Is it my fault?"

"No, it's not your fault. It's mine."

"Did you guys have a fight or something?"

"Yes, I'm afraid we did. I hope we can work things out, but right now it doesn't look too promising."

Again she fell silent for a few moments. Then she said, "I'm sorry, Dad."

"Yeah. Me, too."

They talked awhile more, then Kaycee's call waiting beeped in, and Brian said he'd let her go. For the remainder of his walk, he thought about what good kids he had. More than anything he wished he could call Susan and tell her what Kaycee had said tonight.

But he knew that wouldn't be possible unless things went the way Brian hoped they'd go when Sasha's case went to court.

The day of Sasha's court date dawned bright and cold. The thermometer had dipped to forty degrees the night before, and even though the sun was shining when they left for the county courthouse that morning, the mercury still hadn't climbed past forty-eight.

Susan had butterflies in her stomach, and she could just imagine how Sasha felt.

Sasha.

Glancing at her sister, who sat in the passenger seat of Susan's car, Susan felt a surge of pride. No one seeing Sasha the night she'd returned home would believe the changes that had taken place in just a couple of months. Today Sasha looked fresh and neat and very attractive. Her hair had recently been cut and was brushed back from her face and curled around her ears. She wore a long black skirt, tailored white blouse and a short black leather jacket. Her makeup was subdued and her only jewelry was a watch with a silver face and black band and small silver earrings.

They didn't talk on the way. Instead they listened to the soft rock station Susan preferred, and Sasha didn't even complain about it, although normally she called the dj's selections elevator music.

They were meeting Stella at the courthouse. She'd prepped Sasha twice in the past week and had pronounced her ready to face the judge.

When they got to the courthouse, they found Stella, looking capable and successful in a beautiful dark-burgundy suit, waiting for them outside the judge's chambers. Stella shook Susan's hand, then turned to Sasha.

"You look great," she said, giving her shoulder a comforting squeeze.

Sasha smiled nervously. "Thanks."

"Take some deep breaths if you're nervous."

Sasha nodded.

"You'll be fine, Sasha," Stella said. She smiled reassuringly.

Susan looked at her watch. It was nine o'clock.

She glanced at the double doors leading to the court. "Should we go in?"

Stella shook her head. "The previous case is still being heard. They'll let us know when it's our turn."

They sat on one of the hard benches lining the walls. Susan watched the other people passing by or waiting outside other courtrooms.

Suddenly she stiffened, and her heart skidded crazily.

Coming down the hall toward them was Brian.

"What's *he* doing here?" Sasha said, fear causing her voice to tremble. She turned to Stella. "Is he going to testify against me?"

"Not that I know of," Stella said. She rose and walked toward Brian.

Susan's heart was pounding so hard she was sure he could hear it. She wished she knew what he and Stella were talking about, but their voices were too low to understand the words. A few minutes later Stella came back to where they were sitting, and Brian—giving Susan one long, enigmatic look— opened the double doors and walked inside the courtroom.

"He said he just came to watch," Stella said. She looked at Susan quizzically.

Susan squirmed under her shrewd gaze. Stella didn't know about Susan's previous relationship with Brian. Even Sasha didn't know the full extent of it, although Susan was sure she'd guessed.

Reaching over, Stella gave Sasha's hand a comforting pat. "He didn't sound as if he was here to sabotage you."

Sasha nodded, but her face was pale.

Susan didn't know what to think. Why *had* Brian come? Surely he knew by now that Sasha was pleading guilty. Was he just curious? Or did he have a darker, ulterior motive? And why did just the sight of him still affect her so strongly?

But she couldn't stew over her questions for very long, because only minutes later people began to pour out of Judge Hawkins's courtroom. When the tide slowed to a trickle, Stella rose, saying, "Let's go."

Susan put a protective arm about Sasha's shoulders. "You okay?"

Sasha nodded, but her face was pale.

Inside, the courtroom looked the same as the others Susan had been in over the years—functional and unlovely. There were about six rows of spectator benches lined up on either side of a central walkway. Beyond was the bar that separated those who came to watch the proceedings and those who were participating in them.

Susan saw that Brian had taken a seat in the last row. There were several other people seated in the various rows, and Susan wondered who they were. She knew she wouldn't be allowed in the inner sanctum unless the judge wanted her to testify in Sasha's behalf, so she took a seat in the first row behind the bar. Stella and Sasha stepped inside where they sat at the table to the left of the judge's desk.

Already seated inside were a court reporter and a bailiff.

Moments later, a brown-haired, youngish man in a rumpled blue suit rushed in, walked through the swinging door and dumped a briefcase on the opposing counsel table. Susan figured that was Joe McCormick, whom Stella had mentioned would be prosecuting.

He'd no sooner taken a seat when a door in the back of the room opened and a fortyish blond woman dressed in black robes walked in. She stepped up to the bench and the bailiff said, "All rise for the Honorable Joanna Hawkins."

Everyone, including Susan, stood.

The judge sat, followed by everyone else. Putting on wire-rimmed glasses, she picked up and scanned some papers, then put them down again. She looked out over the courtroom. Susan's heart fluttered like a hummingbird as the judge's gaze rested on Sasha. "I see that all parties are here," she said. Turning, she nodded to the prosecutor. "Mr. McCormick. What have we here?"

He stood, smoothing down his jacket. Looking over to Stella and Sasha, he said, "Your Honor, the defendant, Sasha Ann Pickering, is accused of fraudulently charging $6,435 to a credit card that did not belong to her. When she was first arrested, she denied involvement in the crime. At her arraignment, she pleaded not guilty. However, her attorney has since advised me that today she intends to change her plea to guilty."

"I figured as much, since we have no jury."

Someone behind Susan tittered at the judge's sarcasm. The judge raised her eyebrows, and the person who found her previous remark amusing fell silent.

Judge Hawkins turned to Stella. "Miss Vogel, nice to see you again."

"Thank you, Your Honor," Stella said, rising.

Then the judge turned her attention to Sasha. "Miss Pickering."

Stella nudged Sasha, who stood, too.

"Yes, Your Honor?" Sasha said.

Susan expelled a breath of relief. She was afraid Sasha would forget what Stella had said about always addressing the judge as "Your Honor."

"Is it true you're changing your plea to guilty?"

"Yes, Your Honor," Sasha said.

"Your Honor," Stella said, "Miss Pickering would like to tell the Court how sorry she is for what she did."

"Go ahead, Miss Pickering," the judge said.

Sasha took a visible breath. "Y-your Honor," she began, her voice quavering slightly, "I am deeply sorry for what I did. I took my sister's credit card and copied down all the information. Then when she was at work, I called the credit card company and changed the address on the card and later I asked for a duplicate to be mailed to the post office box number that I gave them. I used the card over the next couple of months and she never knew because the statements went to the new address."

"And why didn't your sister wonder about the statements?" Judge Hawkins asked.

It surprised Susan that the judge would interrupt and ask a question, but neither Stella nor the prosecutor seemed to think it was odd.

"Because, Your Honor, she never used the card, so she didn't have an outstanding balance," Sasha said, her voice much stronger now.

"I see," the judge said. "And how does your sister feel about what you did to her?"

"She…she's been wonderful, Your Honor. If I were in her shoes, I'd hate me, but she doesn't. She's disappointed in me, I know, but she hasn't abandoned me. She arranged for my bail, and she's paying for my attorney, and she's here with me today."

"And how do *you* feel about what you did to her, young lady?" the judge said.

"I'm so ashamed," Sasha said. "M-my sister trusted me, and I betrayed her. My sister raised me, Your Honor, after our mother died when I was eleven. She's always stood behind me, no matter how much trouble I've given her. She's such a good person. What I wish more than anything is that I could be like her."

Susan dug a tissue out of her purse and dabbed at

her eyes. She ached for Sasha and hoped the judge recognized the honesty and truth of her words.

"Miss Vogel, please call Miss Pickering's sister. I have some questions for her."

Susan immediately stood, and Stella motioned her forward. Once inside the bar, Susan stood next to Stella.

"Your Honor," Stella said, "this is Susan Pickering, Sasha's older sister."

"Miss Pickering," the judge said, addressing Susan, "tell me how you feel about what your sister did and what you think should happen to her now."

Susan took a deep breath. "I wish she hadn't done it, Your Honor, but she did. I'm encouraged that she's so genuinely ashamed of herself and sorry about the pain she caused me. I'm also encouraged because she's trying so hard to be responsible, and for the first time in many years, she's working diligently to make up for her mistakes. I—I hope you'll give her another chance."

"Thank you, Miss Pickering."

Susan wasn't sure if she should stay there or not, and her expression must have shown that indecision, because the judge said, "You may return to your seat."

Susan walked back to the outer area. Before sitting down again, she glanced to the back of the courtroom. Brian was still there. She wondered what he was thinking. Did he think she was a fool to defend Sasha?

"You may be seated, too," Judge Hawkins said, nodding to Stella and Sasha. Turning to the prosecutor, she said, "Mr. McCormick, what is your recommendation?"

"Your Honor," Joe McCormick said, standing, "because this is a first offense and because the defendant seems truly remorseful, I am recommending leniency in this case, although I do believe some punishment is necessary due to the serious nature of the crime. I also believe counseling should be part of the defendant's sentence."

Judge Hawkins nodded. She rubbed the bridge of her nose, consulted the papers on her desk again, then stared out into space for what seemed like hours to Susan. Finally she sighed and turned back to Sasha. "Will the defendant please stand?" she said.

Stella and Sasha rose. Stella's hand lay lightly on Sasha's back, more for emotional support, Susan knew, than for anything physical.

"Miss Pickering, I do believe that you are very sorry for what you did," Judge Hawkins said, "and I also believe you've learned a hard lesson and will never do anything similar again. In fact, it seems to me that you've already begun to turn your life around. However, the fact remains that, first offense or not, your crime *was* serious. You defrauded your sister's credit card company out of a great deal of money. As I'm sure your attorney told you, I could sentence you to as much as ten years in prison as well as fine you the sum of ten thousand dollars."

Susan gasped. Ten years! Stella had said five years was the maximum. *Please, God, no…*

Judge Hawkins looked at Sasha for a long moment. Susan knew Sasha was terrified, but she kept her head up and returned the judge's gaze steadily.

"Considering your age and lack of previous charges," Judge Hawkins said, "I am hereby sentencing you, Sasha Ann Pickering, to a probationary term of three years, the first six months of which will be served in the Banning Halfway House for Women. During your probation, you will receive counseling and you will do community service that will be assigned by your probation officer and your counselor. You will follow the rules of your probation as they are set up for you, and you will follow all the rules of the halfway house. Should you break any of these terms, you will immediately be transferred to the state prison for women and will serve out the remainder of your sentence there. Do you understand this sentence?"

"Yes, Your Honor," Sasha said.

"Yes, Your Honor, she does," Stella said.

"Additionally," the judge said, "when you have finished fulfilling the terms of your sentence, you will work out a plan with the court whereby you will begin to pay back the sum you stole—" She gave Sasha a stern look. "For you *did* steal the money. You will make these payments each month until the entire amount is paid back. Is that clear?"

"Yes, Your Honor," Sasha said.

"You—not your sister."

"I understand, Your Honor."

"Good."

Susan felt weak with relief. A halfway house! And only thirty minutes away in Banning. She wanted to run up to the judge and kiss her, she was so grateful.

"Your Honor?" Sasha said. "Thank you."

For the first time since she'd entered the court, the judge smiled. "You're welcome, Sasha. Don't let me down."

"I won't, Your Honor."

Judge Hawkins banged her gavel, then rose and left the courtroom.

Stella was beaming as she turned around to face Susan. Susan looked at Sasha. Their expressions said everything. It was a bittersweet moment for Susan. She knew Sasha had many hard moments ahead of her. The halfway house wouldn't be a luxury hotel, by any means, but it wasn't prison. There would be no bars on the windows, and she wouldn't be in the company of hardened criminals. The other women in the halfway house would be more like her, women who had made mistakes but could be rehabilitated.

When Stella and Sasha joined Susan, the sisters hugged. Susan also hugged Stella, saying, "Thank you so much."

"It wasn't me. It was Sasha and the judge," Stella said.

"We couldn't have done it without you," Susan insisted. She knew what they owed the attorney. No amount of money could ever pay her for what she'd accomplished for them.

"Like the judge said, Sasha," Stella said, "don't disappoint me."

"I won't, I promise you. W-when do I have to go to the halfway house?"

"Let's go find out," Stella said.

While Stella and Sasha talked to Joe McCormick, Susan wondered once again what Brian was thinking. She desperately wanted to talk to him. And if he gave any indication at all that he wanted to talk to her, she would make the first move and go back there.

But when she turned around, he was gone.

Chapter Thirteen

Everywhere Susan looked, she saw signs of Christmas. Downtown, the streets had garlands of greenery and lights strung across them, and all the shop windows were decorated with holly, lights, angels, trees, Santas, gaily wrapped boxes and nativity scenes. The village square looked magnificent, with the bandstand and the huge spruce tree in the center twinkling with hundreds of lights both day and night.

Susan had made an effort to make her shop look festive, but this year her heart really wasn't in it. She knew the holidays would be hard, with Sasha at the halfway house and Brian out of her life.

She was just grateful she had her friends. On

Christmas eve, Susan would be singing at her church for the early service. Afterward she and Ann and Carol planned to have dinner together. Shawn had invited all three of them—the homeless, they joked—to celebrate Christmas Day with her and her family, but Susan was planning to spend the day with Sasha and the others at the halfway house.

She sighed.

Sasha had asked for permission to come home on Christmas Day, but her probation officer had said it was against the rules. Both sisters had hoped she would relax the rule about not leaving the halfway house unless it was for the assigned community service or a death in the family, but she hadn't.

Susan wondered what Brian would be doing for Christmas. She imagined he would have the girls for part of the day and they would all be at his parents' with the rest of his family. Would she have been there, too—at least for the part of the day she wasn't with Sasha—if they hadn't broken up? Would his family have accepted her by now?

She wondered if he ever thought of her. And if he did, did his heart ache the way hers did?

She had caught a glimpse of him one day when she was leaving the parking lot of the supermarket and he was driving in. She didn't think he'd seen her; he wasn't looking in her direction. Just that little glimpse had caused her chest to hurt and had brought tears to her eyes.

God, she was a mess!

You'd think, after three months, she'd be over him. But the pain she felt when she remembered their times together was still as strong as it had been the night she told him not to come back.

Why did you listen to me? her heart cried, even as she knew the reason. He'd listened because down deep he came to realize they weren't right for each other. He'd thought about how his girls had reacted to her. Then he'd thought about how his daughters would be exposed to Sasha, a convicted criminal, if he married Susan. And he'd felt relief that he'd escaped from making a very bad mistake.

She tried not to think about Brian, but that was like trying not to breathe. Sooner or later you had to take a breath.

But time heals everything, she told herself. She'd survived her father's death and then her mother's.

She would survive this, too.

"This is weird, Dad, you know?"

Brian chuckled at Kaycee's observation. The two of them were sitting together at the reception celebrating Lonnie's marriage. It might seem weird to other people, but he was glad Lonnie had invited him to her wedding. It had given him a twinge to see her walk up the aisle of the small nondenominational chapel she and Ethan had chosen, but it didn't last long.

Mostly he was just envious that she'd found someone and that everything had worked out well for them.

He didn't want to think about Susan, but it was impossible not to. She should be here with him. They should be planning their *own* wedding.

Would that ever happen?

Or was it truly over?

Brian didn't know. He only knew he didn't want to imagine what his future would be like if Susan wasn't a part of it.

At two o'clock in the afternoon on the Sunday before Christmas, Susan pulled into the parking lot of the Banning Halfway House for Women. She smiled when she saw the snowman someone had made in the front yard. This one even had a corncob pipe in his mouth. Where had they *ever* found that?

The Maple Hills–Banning area had had their first really significant snowfall of the year during the night, and today more was predicted.

Susan loved snow. She didn't even mind shoveling her driveway; it was good exercise. As she walked up the front sidewalk, her breath plumed out in front of her.

Reaching the porch of the large brick and frame house, she rang the doorbell. A few moments later, Linda Kaminsky, the director of the house, released the lock and opened the door. "Hi, Susan."

"Hi, Linda." Susan liked the director. A no-nonsense woman who had been a high-powered executive until she'd lost her daughter to crack cocaine, she really cared about the women who came to her and her staff. "Where's Eddie today?" Eddie Jamison was the day shift security guard.

Linda smiled. "Back in the kitchen helping to decorate Christmas cookies."

Susan smiled, too. She also liked Eddie, an ex-football player who was there more for the girls' protection than he was to keep them from leaving. In fact, they could leave at any time. There was nothing to stop them except the knowledge that, in the end, breaking the rules would only bring them harsher punishment.

"Sasha's back there, too," Linda said.

Susan started for the kitchen, but Linda put a hand on her arm.

"I have some good news for you. Thelma told me she's changed her mind and has now given permission for Sasha to come home Christmas Day as long as you have her back here by nine o'clock."

"Oh, Linda, that's *wonderful!*" Susan said, beaming. "Oh, she'll be so thrilled."

Linda nodded. "I haven't told her yet. I figured you'd want to do that." She grimaced. "It's a little touchy because some of the others asked for permission to go home for the day, too, and Thelma has denied all of them except Sasha and Karen."

Karen Lenska was Sasha's best friend at the halfway house. They were close in age, and Karen's crime was similar in nature to Sasha's. Susan had mixed feelings about Karen. She was glad Sasha had a friend here, for she knew her sister needed someone to talk to, but she worried that maybe Karen wasn't as determined as Sasha was to turn her life around.

"You know, we're really proud of Sasha," Linda said. "She's doing a magnificent job at the center. They love her there. In fact, Margaret Hobson told me she thinks Sasha would make a terrific counselor."

Susan smiled. Sasha's community service assignment had been to work with the girls at Safe Haven, a shelter for teenage girls in trouble. She'd been there for five weeks now, and whenever she and Susan talked, Sasha bubbled over with enthusiasm for the place.

"They're doing such good things there," she'd said just last week. "It's a fantastic place, Susan." Then her expression saddened. "You wouldn't believe the stories I've heard, Susan. Some of the girls have been abused. Others grew up with drug-addicted parents. Just horrible stories. It's made me realize all the more how lucky I was to have had you after Mom died."

Susan had gotten a lump in her throat when Sasha said that. It made all the tough times fade away.

"I'll wait to tell her when we're alone," she said now.

Linda nodded.

Entering the kitchen, Susan was assailed with the aroma of baking cookies. Five women and a laughing Eddie looked up. Sasha grinned. "Hey, sis. Look what we're doing!" She held up a Christmas-tree-shaped cookie she was decorating.

"Pull up a chair, Susan," said Karen Lenska. "We can use another pair of hands."

Susan greeted everyone, then sat down. For the next hour, she helped ice and decorate cookies. The banter between the women was infectiously joyful. It was obvious they were enjoying the break from routine and the approach of the holidays, although Susan wondered how long that happiness would last when the big day arrived and they couldn't spend it at home with their loved ones.

When the last cookie was decorated, Susan and Sasha, mugs of hot tea in hand, headed for the common room where several areas had been screened off for privacy.

"Guess what?" Susan said when they were seated.

Sasha clapped her hand over her mouth and her eyes rounded in surprise when Susan told her about her probation officer's decision. "Oh, Susan! I'm so happy!" She threw her arms around Susan and hugged her.

"I'm happy, too, honey."

"So what shall we do? Are you going to cook a turkey?"

"No. Shawn has invited us both to come to her house for dinner. And yes, she's doing a turkey. I'll bake pies."

"Banana cream?"

Susan laughed. Banana cream pie had been their mother's specialty and she'd made it for all holidays. Now Susan always carried on the tradition. "Yes, of course. And pumpkin."

"The only thing is…"

"What?"

Sasha's smile faded. "I wish I could buy gifts for everyone. I can't even buy *you* anything."

"Sasha, that's not important. The important thing is we'll be together."

Sasha sighed. "I know."

"When you're finished here and you get a paying job, then you'll be able to buy Christmas presents. *Not* on my credit card, though." She grinned to show she was teasing.

Sasha laughed. "Don't worry. I never want to even *see* another credit card. If I can't afford to pay cash, I don't intend to buy it." Then she sobered. "Sissy, there's something I have to tell you."

For just a moment Susan's heart plunged. Was Sasha in some kind of trouble that Susan didn't know about? But just as quickly as the thought formed, Susan pushed it away. She knew it was unworthy of her.

"I promised him I wouldn't say anything to you, but I have to."

What in the world was she talking about?

"Because," Sasha continued, "it's my fault you guys are no longer together."

Susan stared at her sister. Brian? Was she talking about *Brian*?

"The thing is, Brian has been visiting me for weeks now, almost from the time I started my sentence. Sometimes he comes here, sometimes he comes to check up on me at the center, and every time he does, we talk."

Susan couldn't believe it. All these weeks? Brian had been visiting Sasha and Sasha hadn't told her?

"He's such a good guy, Susan. You know, I hated him when he arrested me, and I was glad you weren't going to see him anymore, but since I've gotten to know him, I realize how selfish and stupid that was. He did me a favor by arresting me. I know that now. Because of him, I have a chance for a good life, one that's productive and helps other people. I have a chance to be like *you*."

Susan was afraid to feel the joy that wanted to erupt inside her. She was afraid if she did, this might turn out to be a dream.

"He loves you, Susan," Sasha said softly. "But he thinks you still hate him."

"I never hated him," Susan whispered around the lump in her throat.

"Then what are you waiting for? Go tell him."

Brian was tired. He'd had another surveillance job that had lasted until midnight, and today, as always, he'd been expected at his parents'. He wondered what would happen if he rebelled and said he'd like an occasional Sunday for himself.

He decided a nice hot shower and a cold beer were in order. After that he'd figure out what, if anything, he felt like eating. Hell, maybe he'd just order in some Chinese. Why not?

He'd barely had time to soap himself when he heard the doorbell. Damn! Who the hell could that be?

He was still debating whether to ignore the bell or rinse off, put his robe on and answer the door when the bell pealed again.

Susan had never been inside Brian's apartment, but she knew exactly where it was, because he'd pointed it out to her once.

She drove carefully on the way there. The streets were slippery with the new snowfall, and the last thing she wanted was to have an accident.

Especially not now.

She couldn't stop smiling. Brian still loved her. He'd been visiting Sasha, and he'd told her he loved her.

Oh, Brian, I'm so sorry I put us both through this.

After what seemed like agonizing hours, but in reality was only forty-five minutes, Susan arrived in Maple Hills. Five minutes later she was pulled up in front of the small apartment complex where Brian lived.

She was half thrilled, half scared, when she saw his Bronco parked in front of his unit.

Slowly, praying he hadn't changed his mind since he'd last talked with Sasha, Susan climbed the stairs to the second floor and rang his doorbell.

She waited, shivering in a sudden blast of wind.

There was no answer.

She rang the bell again.

And waited.

And waited.

She was just about to leave in disappointment—maybe he'd gone somewhere in someone else's car—when she heard the dead bolt being released.

The door opened, and Brian—barefoot, hair wet, wearing a terry cloth robe—stared at her in open-mouthed surprise. Then his entire face lit up. "Susan!"

Susan's eyes filled with tears. "Hello, Brian."

Still he stared at her, as if he couldn't believe she was actually there.

Then, in a moment she knew she would take out and treasure the rest of her life, he reached for her. As his strong arms enfolded her, and his mouth dipped to capture hers in a kiss that said everything, she knew no matter how many problems they might have to deal with, as long as they loved each other, they would work them out.

Eighteen Months Later

"I heard from Sasha today."

Brian looked up from the newspaper. The two of them were sitting in the sunporch that Brian had built onto the back of Susan's home—which was now *their* home. He smiled. "What did she have to say?"

"She loves her classes and she loves her job." Susan smiled, setting aside her knitting. Recently she and

Ann had taken knitting classes, and Susan was really enjoying her new skill. "And she's met someone."

Brian drank some of his iced tea and lowered the paper. "A guy?"

Susan laughed. "Yes. A guy."

"What kind of a guy? Who is he? What does he do?"

"You know, Brian, sometimes I think you're more like her father than her brother-in-law."

"Don't give me a hard time, Susan. Just tell me about this guy, okay? He'd better be good enough for her."

Susan couldn't help it; she laughed again. But she loved that Brian felt so protective of Sasha. Things could have been so different. He could have resented his sister-in-law for all the grief she'd caused the two of them in the early stages of their romance; instead he had grown to love Sasha as much as Susan did, and he worried about her more. He said it was because he knew more about the perils of the world than Susan did, but Susan knew his feelings went much deeper than that. *I am so lucky,* she thought for at least the thousandth time.

"His name is Josh Kimble and he's a senior." Susan smiled. "Next year he'll be in medical school. He's already been accepted. He wants to be a pediatrician."

Brian frowned. "What's the catch?"

"What do you mean, catch?"

"He sounds too good to be true."

Susan shook her head. "You're impossible."

"Does he know about Sasha's past?"

"She said she's told him everything, and he doesn't care. She said he's proud of the way she's turned her life around and really proud of the work she's doing with troubled girls."

"He *is* too good to be true," Brian pronounced.

"She wants to bring him home next weekend for us to meet him."

"The girls will be here next weekend, you know."

"I know. Sasha said she wants Josh to meet them, too."

That was another thing that continually amazed Susan—the way Brian's daughters and Sasha got along like a house afire. Kaycee thought Sasha was cool and sophisticated, and Janna admired the work she did. She, in turn, felt protective of them and constantly warned them about falling in with bad company or blaming their problems on their parents.

"That's not all the news I have," Susan said softly.

Brian, who had returned to reading the paper, lowered it again, perhaps alerted by the change in her voice. He looked at her quizzically.

"I went to the doctor today," Susan said.

Now he frowned. "Is something wrong?"

She smiled secretly and reached into the large quilted bag where she kept her yarn and knitting supplies. Removing a plastic bag, she unzipped it and took out a tiny pair of yellow booties. She held them up.

She knew the moment he realized what she was

telling him. Throwing aside the paper, he came to where she was sitting and knelt before her. His blue eyes— she so loved his eyes!—were shining. "Susan? Are you saying what I think you're saying?" he whispered.

Damn. Why did she *always* cry when she was happy? She nodded. "Yes. I'm six weeks pregnant."

Now *his* eyes looked suspiciously shiny.

"Oh, Brian, you're happy about it, aren't you?"

"You nut. Of course I'm happy. In fact, if I was any happier, I don't think I could stand it." Then, rising, he pulled her up into his arms.

When he kissed her, she thought, *I'm the luckiest woman in the world,* for the thousand and first time.

* * * * *

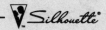

SPECIAL EDITION™

PRESENTING A NEW MINISERIES BY

RaeANNE THAYNE:

The Cowboys of Cold Creek

BEGINNING WITH

LIGHT THE STARS

April 2006

Widowed rancher Wade Dalton relied
on his mother's help to raise three small
children—until she eloped with "life coach"
Caroline Montgomery's grifter father! Feeling
guilty, Caroline put her Light the Stars
coaching business on hold to help the angry
cowboy…and soon lit a fire in his heart.

DON'T MISS THESE ADDITIONAL BOOKS IN THE SERIES:

DANCING IN THE MOONLIGHT, May 2006
DALTON'S UNDOING, June 2006

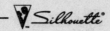

SPECIAL EDITION™

DON'T MISS THE FIRST BOOK IN
PATRICIA McLINN's
EXCITING NEW SERIES
Seasons in a Small Town

WHAT ARE FRIENDS FOR?
April 2006

When tech mogul Zeke Zeekowsky
returned for his hometown's Lilac Festival,
the former outsider expected a hero's
welcome. Instead, his high school fling,
policewoman Darcie Barrett, mistook him
for a wanted man and handcuffed him!
But the software king and the small-town
girl were quick to make up....

SPECIAL EDITION™

THE THIRD STORY IN

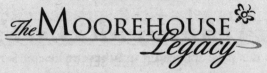

A family tested by circumstance,
strengthened by love.

FROM THE FIRST

April 2006

Alex Moorehouse had loved Cassandra Cutler
from the first. Then she'd been his best friend's
wife. Now she was a widow, which, for Alex,
didn't change anything. Cassandra was still
off-limits. And he was still a man who loved
no one but her.

A 4–1/2–star Top Pick!
"A romance of rare depth,
humor and sensuality."
—*Romantic times BOOKclub* on
BEAUTY AND THE BLACK SHEEP, the
first in *the Moorehouse Legacy*

A forty-something blushing bride?

Neely Mason never expected to walk down the aisle, but it's happening, and now her whole Southern family is in on the event. Can they all get through this wedding without killing each other? Because one thing's for sure, when it comes to sisters, *crazy* is a relative term.

The

GOOD KIND OF CRAZY

TANYA MICHAELS

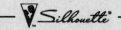

SPECIAL EDITION™

RETURN TO HART VALLEY IN

HER BABY'S HERO

BY

KAREN SANDLER

Elementary school teacher Ashley Rand
was having CEO Jason Kerrigan's baby.
Even though they came from different
worlds, each was running from trouble.
So when Jason rented the Victorian house
of Ashley's dreams, they both believed life
would slow down. Until they found out
Ashley was having twins!

Available April 2006
at your favorite retail outlet.

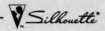

SPECIAL EDITION™

THE LAST COWBOY

BY

CRYSTAL GREEN

Felicia Markowski wants children
more than anything, but her infertility
is an obstacle she cannot overcome.
But when she meets handsome cowboy
Jackson North—a brooding man with a
past—she wonders if fate has other plans
for her after all.

Look for this story
April 2006.

COMING NEXT MONTH